I0638409

DEATH AND THE DIVA

SAM CHEEVER

ELECTRIC PROSE PUBLICATIONS

"You have that essential Je ne sais quoi that it takes to tell a story so mesmerizing you cannot stop reading once started. You are not telling stories to your readers...you are taking them with you on your adventures so that the experience can be shared by all as it happens and not simply replayed like a memory on the page of a diary! You are indeed gifted and it is my pleasure to read your books!"

Valerie Irwin

Maybell never expected to bump into her high school drama rival again. But May's old nemesis has apparently been taking acting lessons. Otherwise, she could never have performed the role of a corpse so convincingly. Oh. Wait...

Asked to take part in a community theatre production for charity, Maybell Ferth thought it would be fun to do something she loved while helping kids in her hometown. But, there was a problem.

Patrice Reynolds had been the bane of May's

existence since high school drama class. When she left community theatre behind, May promised herself she'd never let the woman get under her skin again. But fate wasn't letting her off the hook that easily.

It was just like Patrice to end up dead in a way that implicated May. Her very public battles with the difficult diva shine a light on May as the number one suspect. The only way to clear her name is to put her professional mourning skills into practice at the funeral. With a murder to solve and her own future at stake, Maybell's acting chops are going to be sorely tested.

STAY IN TOUCH

Sam doesn't give away a lot of books. But she values her readers and, to show it, she's gifting you a copy of a fun book just for signing up for her newsletter!

SIGN UP HERE: https://samcheever.com/newsletter

1

Imagine my surprise when I walked out onto the stage and saw that someone had left the spotlight on. The sight hit me like a French dessert, a rolling wave of rich chocolate, melting my brain for just a moment. Every pleasure center I had fired at the sight.

A spotlight...my drug of choice.

I'd thought the theatre was empty. In fact, I'd deliberately timed my arrival to pick up my copy of the script, hoping the place *would* be empty.

Call me a coward if you want. I wouldn't blame you for it. But since learning that my arch-nemesis, Patrice Reynolds was directing the play I'd happily agreed to take part in, I'd been struggling with bowing out, exiting stage left, shuffling off to Buffalo.

The spotlight grew closer, and I looked down to discover that my feet were moving toward it. It was as if someone had taken the proverbial stage hook to my middle and was reeling me in.

That someone, of course, was me, MayBell Ferth, thirty-three-year-old professional mourner and sometimes thespian. I'd walked away from a very satisfying career in community theatre because I have a diva allergy. In fact, I was allergic to almost everything having to do with acting, except for the actual performances themselves.

Dealing with massive egos and infighting had sucked the love of theatre right out of me. It had given me angst.

And Patrice Reynolds had been the cause of much of that angst.

Patrice and I had been competing for prime roles since high school when she'd shoved me down a short flight of stairs hoping I'd break something to keep me from getting the coveted lead as Tinkerbell in Peter Pan.

Unfortunately for Patrice, I come from a long line of Ferths with good bones. Even more unfortunately for her, Mrs. Mike, the drama teacher, witnessed the dastardly deed and punished Patrice by giving her the worst role in the play. The crocodile.

It took Patrice all of junior year and most of senior year to recover from the humiliation. To this day, she still jumps and gives a little scream when she hears a ticking clock.

But anyway, that's ancient history. Except, not really. Patrice still hates the sight of me—I nailed the Tinkerbell role to much acclaim— and I still shudder at the thought of working with her.

I stopped at the edge of the spotlight and looked around, wondering who'd left the light on and why. Had someone been practicing lines? I hadn't seen anyone when I came into the building. Patrice's assistant, Manny, had left my copy of the script behind stage, but he wasn't there.

It had been an exhausting day, and all I wanted was to go home to my cozy little apartment and spring my adorable little fluffball, Shakespeare, from his kennel. I fully planned to spend my evening snuggling Shakes and eating pizza.

A flicker of movement drew my gaze to the shadows bathing the back of the theatre. I hesitated, glancing that way and seeing nothing. Shaking my head, I gave the spotlight one last adoring glance before spinning on my heel. I needed my furbaby and a glass of red wine more than I needed that spotlight fix.

I headed backstage, my footsteps quick and determined. Having made the decision to go home, I was suddenly anxious to leave.

As I stepped off the stage, I jolted to a stop. A cable swayed above my head as if someone had just bumped it. I stood staring at the swinging cable, listening.

The building was silent.

The click of a switch being thrown cast the stage behind me into darkness.

My heart kicked into panic mode.

There was a swishing sound, and my instincts told me to step back into the heavy, velvet drapes surrounding the stage. Breathing as quietly as I could, given that my heart was pounding out a frantic bass beat, I focused on listening. Somewhere in the distance, a clock ticked. I thought of Patrice's reluctant crocodile, and a nervous bark of laughter escaped my lips before I could stop it.

Footsteps exploded in my direction. The curtains attacked me, wrapping me in a smothering embrace. I swung my arms in panic.

My fist hit something fleshy, and I kicked in that direction. Unfortunately, the heavy drapes kept me from doing much more than grazing my assailant. I fought the dusty air, trying to breathe through the panic.

The dust was choking. When I sucked air to scream, I got a mouth full of velvet and some kind of fiber lodged in my throat.

A violent coughing fit added to my troubles.

As my coughing eased, I could hear heavy, wheezing breaths, as if someone else was having trouble breathing through the dust. Suddenly, the curtains relinquished their hold on me. Footsteps pounded rapidly away.

Panting from fear, I tried to cough up the fiber while fighting my way out of my drapery prison. Once clear, I stumbled in the direction of the nearest light switch, smacking my shin on something along the way.

"Ouch, ouch, ouch!"

Finding the switch, I flipped it. Several lights came on with a thud. I spun to look for my attacker and found something worse.

Much worse.

A chalk-white face stared blankly at me from beneath the curtains I'd gotten tangled in. One foot, long and narrow and encased in a soft ballet flat, stuck out of the drapery.

Too pale blue eyes were wide, radiating terror even after death. Blood slipped down the woman's temple, tangling in the long, curly golden locks she'd always been so vain about. More blood stained the front of her silk blouse.

One hand protruded from a fold in the heavy, crimson drapes. The fingers were bent, two of the fingernails torn and bloody.

For a long moment, I just stared at the woman, knowing it was too late to call for help. And then I sighed, pulling my cell phone out of my pocket and hitting a button from my recent call list.

"Yo, ho, ho," said a deep voice on the other end of the call. "What's up?"

"Argh," I said, dreading the next words I'd need to speak. "I found a dead body. It's Patrice Reynolds."

My brother sighed, long and loud. "Where are you."

I wasn't quite sure how to react as I watched the police and crime people swarm all over the scene. As a professional mourner, it could be said that I was used to dead bodies. However, my variety of dead person was generally tidier, without the horror movie ambiance that poor Patrice was currently exhibiting.

"Okay, pipsqueak," Argh said condescendingly as he strode in my direction. "Tell me how you happened to be the one who found the victim."

"Victim? So, you're saying she was murdered?" I asked my brother, determined to get as much information from him as he was going to take from me.

"I'm the one asking the questions," he began.

"And, I'll answer them. Every single one," I assured him. "But I think, since I was the unfortunate schmoe who stumbled over the body, I deserve to know what happened. In a way, *I'm* a victim too."

He snorted. "Nice try. What you are, McMay-Beth," he told me sarcastically, "is a suspect. Now spill."

"Come on, you don't really think I killed her?" I

straightened my shoulders, plastered an indignant expression on my face, and flavored it with just a tiny bit of offense for good measure. I'd say it was some of my finest work, but that wouldn't have taken into account my audience.

Argh was a tough sell. The toughest of my siblings and even tougher than the Lieutenant. As a cop, Argh had dealt with liars his entire career. Good liars. Better than I was. The only thing I had in my favor was the fact that he loved me like a brother. Because he was one.

Still, I rarely managed to float a prevarication past him.

He laughed at me. Actually laughed. The laugh even reached his eyes.

The rat.

"Try again, Drama Diva. You have a long history with the deceased. By your own admission, you hated her."

I held up a hand. "I didn't say that. When did I say I hated the *victim*?" I emphasized the word to remind him that he should never have given away the fact that Patrice was murdered.

"Let's see," Argh responded. "In fifth grade, you stomped into the house and threw yourself onto the couch, face down, screaming, and I quote, 'I hate Patrice Reynolds!'"

I glared at him. Nobody should have such perfect recall. A young girl depends on the people around her to have short memories. It's vital for our emotional health at that age to feel our loved ones aren't cataloging our mistakes and tantrums. "I was in fifth grade. Cut me some slack. At that age, you were still rockin' a mohawk."

He winced but wasn't deterred from his mission. "In your sophomore year, you threatened to, and I quote again, 'Wedgie her with her thong until she gasped out her last breath.'"

I hated that my lip was sticking out like I was a petulant child, but I seemed unable to control it. "I'm pretty sure exigent circumstances would have bought me a pass in a court of law."

Argh shook his head. "Sorry McBethBell. If the legal system made a habit of exonerating females for performing death-wedgies on the women their boyfriends slept with behind their backs, your species would cease to exist within a year."

"She slept with my boyfriend and then bragged about it," I said, looking for clemency.

"Nope." He pulled out his notebook. "You are hereby declared a person of interest."

I snorted. "There's no such thing as hereby declaring."

"I just invented it. Now, tell me what happened here tonight."

Blowing out a frustrated breath, I slumped. "I have no idea what happened. All I did was come in to grab my copy of the script."

He jotted that down. "Go on."

"I grabbed my script."

"Where was it?"

I pointed to a table near the exit.

He made a point of looking from the table to the corpse, twenty feet away, and arched a dark brow.

I really wanted to smack him. But, even the exigent circumstance of him being a pain in my behind wouldn't save me from the Lieutenant if I did. I could hear my father's disappointed voice in my mind. He'd tell me I must always respect the law. Even when it was my brother. "I noticed that the stage spot was on and came to investigate."

His pencil stopped moving over his pad. Both brows lifted, and his lips twitched. "You stood under the spotlight, didn't you?"

"I really hate you," I told him.

He chuckled with glee. "I notice the light is off now. Did you turn it off?"

"No."

He stared at me.

"I didn't. It just went off."

"It just went off? By itself?"

I shrugged. "Maybe the guy I heard running away turned it off."

Argh stilled, his expression slowly transforming to one of sheer disbelief, and then he dropped his head and sighed. "MayBell, I swear..."

"What's going on?" a familiar voice said from

across the room. I knew that voice. I hadn't heard it for a while. A long while.

When Argh and I both turned to Eddie Deitz, he jolted to a stop, his hands lifting to protect himself from the Hell our mutual glares promised.

2

——————

"I ...uh...hey, May." He laughed nervously. "That rhymed, didn't it?"

Argh and I glared at the way-too-good-looking man standing three yards away, his hands still up as if to fend off an attack. "How's it going?"

Argh lifted a dark brown brow. "How's it going? Are you brain-damaged? Why haven't you called my sister for an entire month?"

I groaned, wishing I could slip beneath the floor and disappear into a puddle. "Argh, is that really the first question we want to ask *Mr. Deitz* right now?"

Argh never shifted his gaze from the handsome traitor across the room. "It is."

"No. It isn't," I disagreed.

"Okay, then how about this? Do you have a death wish showing up right now?" Argh asked Deitz. "Did you think you could just waltz right back into May's life like you didn't dump her on her backside after she saved you from a murder charge?"

I wilted downward, wondering what my chances for turning into that puddle were.

"I...huh?" Deitz said, frowning. "Murder charge? I was never a serious suspect."

"Weren't you?" my brother asked. "Maybe you'd like to accompany me to the station so we can talk about it. I'm pretty sure the Lieutenant would love to chat with you for a while. There's probably a cell there with your name on it."

To his credit, Deitz didn't pale or run for his life. But I did hear him swallow kind of loudly.

I shook my head, envying Ant-Man for his ability to shrink from view. "What are you doing here, Deitz?"

His gaze slid to me, changing, warming. "Hey, May..." he stopped, sighed, and shook his head. "Sorry, I'm not usually such a dufus."

"Aren't you?" Argh asked.

I touched my brother's arm. "Can you give us a minute, please?"

"Nope," Argh said, crossing his arms over his chest.

"Argh," I warned.

He shook his head.

"Just one minute. Sixty short seconds."

He looked into my eyes, and I let him see the

hurt in my gaze. I allowed tears to swim in my eyes and my lip to quiver with pain.

It only took a minute. I saw the exact moment he softened. He squeezed my shoulder and strode past Deitz, close enough to bump him aside as he passed with a glower.

Deitz lifted his hands and stepped back. Then, he turned a cautious smile to me. "Wow, he's intense."

The smile died when he saw my expression.

I stepped closer, poking an angry finger into Deitz's breastbone. "You dare to show up now? After almost four weeks of silence? And why *did* you show up here? Are you following me?"

Yeah, the quivering lip and tears had been fake. Argh should have known that, but I was glad he hadn't.

Deitz rubbed the spot on his chest that my finger had been abusing. "First of all," he said, gently taking my finger into his warm, lightly calloused hand to stop the abuse. "I'm not following you. I didn't even know you were here. I came to pick up my client."

My stomach clenched at his warm touch, and I jerked my finger out of his grip. "What client?"

"I'll tell you," Eddie said, stepping closer. He looked down at me, his forest green gaze dark with emotion. "But first, let me explain about not calling you."

I shook my head, backing away from him. "Nope," I said, channeling Argh. "I'm not interested in your excuses. Just tell me who your client is."

"Yeah," Argh said, handing me a plastic cup filled with water. "I'd like to know who that is too."

"Thanks," I told him, taking a drink of the cool liquid. It felt like heaven on my dry throat. "There's nobody here except the victim and me," I said. "According to you, I'm not the reason you're here. So were you here to see the victim?" My tone brimmed with accusation.

"I can't tell you that..." Eddie started to say.

Argh bristled, stepping close with a threatening look. "You can, and you will, Deitz."

"If you'd just let me finish," Eddie said. "I can't tell you if I came to see the victim because I don't know who the victim is."

Argh and I shared a "Do you believe this guy?" look. Just a step up from a dual eye roll. We both turned to him and crossed our arms, looking like the community theatre version of Men in Black...minus the black. And the sunglasses. Okay, we looked nothing like Men in Black. But I really wanted us to.

"What's with the matching scowls?" Deitz asked. "I'm not playing games here, guys. I came to pick up my client. From this setup..." He waved a hand over the uniformed cops and the body in the black bag that was currently making its way out the door toward a waiting ambulance. "I'm starting to suspect that your victim and my client might be one and the same."

Argh and I both elevated a brow in silent question.

Eddie scowled back at us. "I always wondered how May could possibly fit into an anal-retentive family of cops. I'm starting to see the resemblance."

"Spill it, Deitz," I told him, losing patience. "Who's your client?"

He sighed. "You first."

"That's it." Argh broke his Men in Black pose to grab the set of cuffs from his pocket. "You're coming down to the station for questioning, Deitz."

"What? Why?"

"Who and where," Argh said. "Now that we have the technical aspects of good communication covered..."

I winced at the sound of the cuffs snapping closed.

"...you can tell me why you murdered Patrice Reynolds." He jerked Eddie toward the door.

Eddie wrenched free. "Wait, what?"

"We already covered that. Try to keep up, Deitz," Argh was enjoying cuffing the PI way too much.

Eddie looked at me as Argh yanked him toward the door. "May, I didn't know she was dead. You have my word on that. She called and asked me to pick her up."

Argh stopped yanking Eddie toward the exit, a smug look on his face.

I rolled my eyes at my brother's tactics, jerking my head toward the cuffs. "Argh."

He gave me a crooked grin and unlocked the bracelets, shoving them back into the pocket of his jeans. "Was it normal for Ms. Reynolds to request that you pick her up?"

Rubbing his wrists, Eddie glowered at Argh. "I can see why you're named for a pirate."

Argh jingled the cuffs inside his pocket. "Yo, ho, ho. Start talking."

"She thought she was being stalked by a fan. That's why she hired me. I've been doing a body-guard slash stalker search assignment for five weeks. When I'm not guarding her, I'm trying to run the stalker to ground." He gave me cow eyes. "It's been exhausting."

Rage burned a path through my belly. "Five weeks? And you didn't tell me?"

"The client asked me not to tell anyone," he said with a shrug. "I was sworn to secrecy."

"Why?" Argh asked.

"I don't know. It was weird. But she'd offered me top dollar to guard her whenever she left her house."

"Why weren't you here tonight then?" I asked, not quite buying his story.

"She said she was meeting an old friend for dinner. He was supposed to pick her up here and bring her home. According to Patrice, she was perfectly safe with the guy. I guess he'd been some hotshot MMA fighter or something."

"But then she called you?" Argh nudged.

"Yeah." Eddie frowned. "Her friend never showed up, and Patrice thought her stalker was in the theatre." He narrowed his gaze on me. "Did you talk to her before she..." He nodded toward the spot where I'd found her body...a spot still marked by a puddle of blood.

"No," I said. "I think she was already dead when I got here. But I might have been almost suffocated by her killer."

"Ixnay on the iller-kay," Argh said in a harsh whisper. "The walls are listening right now."

I glanced around and saw that several people were indeed listening to our conversation. "Maybe we should shoo them all out until we process the scene."

"We?" Argh asked. "I hope you're having delusions of grandeur and are using that as the royal *we,* 'cause you won't be processing squat here."

"Argh," I said, my tone irritated. "I found the body. I should be included."

He shook his head and pointed to the door. "Out. I'll talk to you two in the morning. I'll probably have more questions by then."

"But..."

"Out."

"I don't think..." Eddie tried.

"Nope. Out."

I barely fought the urge to stick my tongue out at the tyrant known as Argh. But I did manage, so I was proud of myself for the restraint. "Fine!" I glared at my brother. "You're going to regret that."

"I don't think so," he said, looking smug.

"Yeah, you are. Because I'm going shopping with Dani next weekend."

Argh turned the color of chalk. "MayBell..."

Dani Kraft was Argh's new sweetie. She was co-owner of a top-notch security company that used to belong to a friend of Deitz's, and she was perfection in a female form. She also had it bad for my brother. But she liked me too, and I was pretty sure I could take some of the shine off the relationship if I told Dani about some things Argh didn't want her to know.

Like about his mohawk phase.

I wouldn't do it, of course. But I was perfectly willing to imply that I would. Seeing my bossy, over-protective brother wriggling on that metaphorical hook made it a pleasant proposition.

I ignored Argh's slightly panicked use of my name and headed toward the exit. "It's too late now, Argh. You've released the Kraken."

3

"MayBell!"

I ignored the deep voice calling my name and hurried to Betty, my aged but beloved car, whose innards were much more capable than her outward appearance would imply.

Deitz caught up without breaking a sweat, his long strides easily outpacing mine. "What exactly is it you just threatened your brother with?"

I slid him a quick, hostile gaze. "Go away, Deitz." I reached for Betty's door, my fingers wrapping around the handle like it had been formed specifically for me. The door creaked when I opened it, but the sound was like a greeting from an old friend.

Deitz's hand clamped down on Betty's doorframe, keeping me from opening it enough to slip inside. "I want to help, May."

I made the gargantuan mistake of looking up into

Eddie's forest green gaze. For just a beat, I fell into that gaze, lost to the man's impossible magnetism.

Eddie Deitz's smoldering good looks were only enhanced by his individual features. He had inky black hair combed straight back from a broad forehead and full lips over nearly perfect white teeth. Only nearly, because one canine was missing the tip as if he'd been punched in the mouth or had fallen on his face. As usual, a dark shadow of whiskers covered his jaw. I wasn't sure if the bristle was intentional or because it was late in the day, but either way, it was sexy. Eddie was a head taller than my own five feet nine and leanly muscled. He wore his usual button-down shirt, pale gray with dark wash jeans that molded his long legs and other attributes like the clothing was crafted specifically for him.

I swallowed hard, blinking myself out of the momentary haze caused by Eddie's nearness and his familiar warm sandalwood scent. "I don't need your help to figure out what happened to Patrice," I told him, though even I realized that the catch in my breath which required me to clear my throat a few times, wasn't very persuasive.

"You do realize you and I are potential suspects, right?"

I skimmed my glance toward the stage door a few feet away. Its scarred and dented profile nearly melted into the brick around it in the sub-par light.

I shivered, realizing the alley where we stood was darker than the street. The nearest street light was broken, and the theatre's security light was on its last legs.

It wasn't a very secure location, which made it a good spot for a killer to strike. Or disappear from sight.

A soft rain started to fall, the moisture lifting the stench of spilled garbage from the dumpster a couple of buildings down. As if refusing to be upstaged, the delicious scent of fried shrimp and spices from Golden Dragon, my favorite Chinese take-out spot, wafted past on a quickening breeze.

"You're cold," Eddie said, drawing my gaze back to him.

I shook my head. "Somebody just walked over my grave, that's all."

He grimaced. "I hate that saying." He pointed to his truck, which was parked under a streetlight half a block away. The glossy black surface glistened under a fresh spate of raindrops. "How about I take you out to dinner? I'd like to explain some things, and we can discuss the murder."

I shook my head, taking advantage of his relaxing grip to pull Betty's door wide. "I'm not interested in your explanations, and I don't need..."

"You don't need my help finding Patrice's killer," he said. "I get it. But do you really think the Lieutenant would sanction you going off alone to find a killer?"

I fought to keep my expression neutral. That right there was dirty pool. "You don't need to worry about what my father thinks. Except for the part where he thinks you're a jerk for not calling me for almost a month."

It was Eddie's turn to wince. He stared off down the alley and nodded. "Fair enough. What if I bring dinner?"

I glanced longingly toward the Dragon, my mouth watering. Was it worth it to be subjected to Eddie's company just for egg rolls and Szechuan chicken? It didn't take me long to answer that question. "Okay, but I don't want to hear your excuses for not calling. That's behind me now. Whatever you and I might have had is over. Understand? I only want to talk about your relationship with Patrice."

He frowned, looking for all the world like he really wanted to argue, but finally nodded. "Deal."

"Yip!"

I opened the door and dropped my keys onto the small table in the foyer.

"Yip! Yip! Yip!"

"I'm coming," I called out, guilt gnawing my

belly as I remembered that poor Shakespeare had been in his kennel, a.k.a. the Pom Hilton, for hours.

"I'm sorry, Shakes. I got tied up at the theatre, and..." I headed into my bedroom and found my little Pomeranian bouncing in front of the kennel door. I knew that bounce. It was a Level 5 jump, seconds away from an explosion of Pom proportions.

I ran to the kennel, wrenched open the door, and stood back as Shakes shot out of there like a cannon-ball from a World War I cannon.

I ran after him, grabbing the front door and yanking it open. "We'll take the stairs!" I yelled in the direction of my dog's frantic, fuzzy backside.

The door opened in the apartment next to mine as Shakes shot toward the stairwell. A disheveled blond dread-head appeared in the opening. "Dude?"

"Shakes has the poops. I need to go."

"Dude!" my next-door neighbor exclaimed.

"I am hurrying. And yes," I called to my mono-syllabic friend as I ran, "I do remember the last time. To his credit, Shakes thought pooping on your news-paper was preferable to soiling the carpet."

That would probably be my fault for newspaper-training him when he was a pup. Besides, he wasn't wrong. In my opinion, despoiling Doug the potted dread-head's paper had been preferable to pooping on the carpet.

However, Doug didn't seem to agree with my assessment.

I hit the stairwell door at a run, slammed my palm into the bar, and followed the fuzzy gray projectile down to the first-floor exit.

Once outside in the cool evening air, Shakes didn't even bother to find the perfect spot to deposit his business. He squatted barely off the sidewalk as I stood huffing and puffing from the headlong rush outside.

Out of habit, I took a deep breath to enjoy the sweet scent of roses, which lined the side of the building. Then grimaced as a natural scent from the opposite end of the spectrum assailed me. "Ugh, Shakes," I said, earning a happy wiggle and a relieved yip from my little dog.

I dug in my pocket for one of the plastic bags I always carried with me and cleaned up the mess, depositing it into a nearby trash can as Shakes meandered around looking for the perfect spot to deposit his other business.

Twenty minutes later, Shakes finally squatted over a carefully-chosen spot of grass. "Thank good-ness," I complained as he bounced back my way.

"Yip!"

"Don't you yip me, little man. I was quite scan-dalized by the way you laid your business down willy-nilly like that," I teased.

"Yip, yip!" he said joyfully. Translation: "Some-times ya gotta live on the edge."

I trudged up the steps behind my jovial little dog,

feeling older than Methuselah next to his energetic self. In the hallway on our floor, Shakespeare took off with a delighted bark, and I looked up to find Deitz talking to a wary Doug in front of my apartment.

My neighbor, whose apartment was currently fogging the air with enough pot smoke to get the entire floor high, might dance to his own drummer on most things, but on one subject he was every bit as traditional and intractable as my bossy brother and overbearing parental unit.

Doug was protective of Shakes and me. In his own way.

As I approached, Doug was shaking his head in disgust that was clearly directed at Deitz. "Dude."

Deitz sighed. "Nobody's ever going to cut me any slack, are they?"

Doug's gaze skimmed my way and tracked me all the way down the hall, no doubt judging my level of surprise at finding Deitz in front of my door. "Dude?" he asked as I arrived.

I shrugged. "He's like a cockroach. He's hard to get rid of."

Doug chuckled huskily, sliding Deitz one last look before shaking his head again. "I'll be watchin' my shows," my neighbor said before disappearing into his apartment again. He stuck his head back out and added, "Scream Hollywood style if you need me."

"Like Janet Leigh in the shower," I promised. As Doug's door closed, I arched a brow at Deitz.

He tensed. "If you won't let me explain, you can't keep treating me like the bad guy."

I laughed. "Nice try." Then the delectable scent of Chinese food wafted over me, and I forgot to be mad.

For the moment.

"I'll give you a half-hour of covert rather than overt judgment."

Deitz shook his head and crouched down to scratch Shakes behind his tiny, perfect ears. "I guess I'll have to live with that."

"Yes, you will." I sailed into my apartment, flinging my keys back onto the table and hanging my damp coat on a hook inside the small coat closet.

Shakes bounded in and blew past me to the kitchen, eyes alight with expectation. I scooped him up some kibble and mixed his favorite soft dog food into it, setting it on the floor and filling his water dish with clean water.

By the time I'd washed my hands, Deitz had the food arrayed on the table and was setting out plates, silverware, and napkins. "Beer?" I asked, my tone cool. The fact that he knew his way around my kitchen and seemed comfortable in it, both irritated and charmed. I was embracing the irritation, knowing that charmed was only going to land me in a Deitz-sized tub of hot water.

"No thanks. Water?"

I narrowed my gaze on him. "No beer?"

My tone was filled with suspicion that, knowing I wasn't a big drinker, Deitz was trying to impress me with his restraint. I held his gaze with my narrowed one for a moment longer, but he refused to bite.

"Do you want me to get it?" he asked, looking confused.

I shook my head and pulled two bottles of water from the fridge.

Shakes had finished his dinner and parked himself next to Eddie's chair, looking up at him with soft, hopeful eyes. I watched in awe as he laid on the canine charm. I'd always said that if my dog ever took a role opposite me on the stage, nobody would even notice I was there. He was the king of softening up a mark, and his adorably sweet act was Oscar-worthy fare.

Deitz finally noticed Shakes and smiled. "That's some Class A begging there, son."

Shakes quivered with excitement. He tapped Deitz's leg with a tiny paw.

Deitz looked at me. "He likes Chinese food?"

I dabbed an eggroll into a small puddle of plum sauce on my plate. "The Lieutenant shares his chicken with Shakes."

Deitz snorted a laugh. "Seriously? He calls him a rodent."

I shrugged. "The Lieutenant believes his man

card will be revoked if he loves a small dog. But Shakes has him totally charmed. If Shakes and I were both caught in a house fire, I'm convinced dad would save Shakes first."

Deitz laughed, holding a piece of Szechuan chicken down for Shakes. The little Pom took the chicken carefully from Deitz's fingers, swallowed it whole, licked his lips, and then patted Deitz's leg again.

"Should I just give him my plate?"

I tried to fight my grin and failed. "Not unless you're signing up for poop duty at midnight."

Deitz's gaze turned all melty and hot. "I can stick around until midnight."

"Well," I murmured. "That went horrifically wrong very quickly."

Deitz chuckled. He took a bite and chewed, a thoughtful look on his too-handsome face. "You know, I'm going to be investigating this anyway. We might as well work together. Otherwise, we'll just get in each other's way."

I knew he was right. I shrugged, noncommittal.

"Two heads are better than one," Deitz added.

I chewed for a minute and then sighed, beaten. "Okay. But it's just work. Nothing else."

Deitz didn't comment on my stipulation, which made me suspicious over whether he'd follow it.

"Tell me about Patrice. Do you know of anybody who might want her dead?"

I made a face. "Honestly, I'm not sure there's anybody in her sphere of acquaintance who hasn't thought about gacking her at least once."

"Gacking her?" Eddie grinned.

I didn't share the grin. "That sphere includes me."

His smile upended. "May, did you kill Patrice?"

I shook my head. "No. But Argh is going to have to take a serious look at me as a suspect." I tapped the end of my eggroll in the plum sauce, my stomach tightening with worry. "That's why I need to find the killer. He's going to be fighting to stay objective on this investigation. And the Lieutenant is going to be in the same boat."

Eddie swallowed a bite of rice and chicken. "You're right. I hadn't thought about that."

I shrugged. "He's never said so, but I'm pretty sure that's why dad has always tried to steer me away from sleuthing." I took a bite of the egg roll. Twisted stomach or not, I never let a good egg roll go to waste. To waist...but not to waste. "I think we can rule out most of the suspects. Patrice was annoying to everyone she came across, especially in her capacity as stage director. The power corrupted her absolutely."

"Okay," Eddie said, giving Shakes another sliver of chicken.

"But just being annoyed isn't really a motive for murder."

"Unless it's a crime of passion. Unplanned. Spur of the moment," Eddie said.

"Right. And I'll admit actors can be mercurial. It's the reason I left the theatre. All that drama and angst made my eyes bulge until I looked like a pug." I frowned thoughtfully. "But for the purposes of isolating our initial layer of suspects, let's set aside the simply irritated and focus on the truly harmed."

He nodded his agreement.

"I think that brings us down to three strong suspects."

"Okay," Eddie said. "That's a manageable number. Let's start there."

4

"Number one," I said, jotting a name into the lined pad of paper in front of me, "Has to be Oscar Miller."

Eddie sat forward, a cold bottle of beer resting on the table in front of him.

"Oscar was an up-and-coming thespian. By all indications, good enough to be headed for Broadway. He had some time in between a play and a minor movie role and offered to join Patrice's very first production."

"Why would he do that?" Eddie asked, seemingly sincere.

"To garner good press in his home town, bolster his reputation for being a good guy, and because he sincerely cares about the kids. Oscar Miller grew up in the system. His drug-addled parents dumped him when he was four years old and never looked back."

Eddie shook his head, brows lowered in a frown. "Sometimes I hate people."

"Ditto," I agreed. "Anyway, Patrice offered Oscar the lead male role in the play. He happily accepted. All was well for about a week. Then the *Asheville Theatre News* published a hit piece on him, basically claiming he was making demands for special publicity, top billing, and a cut of any money raised for the orphanage."

"Was he making demands?" Eddie asked.

"Not that I'm aware of. I met the guy, Deitz. I remember thinking he was too kind to survive in the acting world."

"Okay, how does Patrice play into it?"

"Oscar Miller insisted from the very first that she was behind the hit piece."

"Let me guess, he rejected her advances?"

I grimaced. "Casting couches apparently work both ways."

He shook his head. "Assume Patrice did leak a hit piece on him. He gets some bad publicity. Isn't the old adage true that there is no bad publicity?"

"Not in this case. The theatre director for his next play is threatening to rescind his offer for the role, claiming Miller was misrepresented to him. Apparently, the man was burned by Diva antics recently and was trying to ensure that his next production was drama-free."

"Good luck with that," Eddie scoffed.

I nodded.

"Does Oscar have any proof that Patrice was the one to burn him?"

"That, I don't know. We'll need to talk to him."

"Okay, interview number one, talk to Oscar Miller. Who else do we have?"

"Jenna Plum."

"Of the Johnson Street Plums?"

I nodded. "She was slated to be stage director for our charity play. Daddy had bought her into the position and everything. But Patrice somehow got the role instead."

"Daddy's little girl wasn't happy?"

"Miss Jenna expects to get everything she wants. And what she wants is to direct theatre. Word is she has aspirations for the big time and viewed our little charity play as the first step in that direction."

"So, applying a whole lot of serendipity to that argument, we're conceivably looking at another case of Patrice ruining a budding career."

"Yep."

"Okay, who's our last suspect?"

"Zeke Hatfield." I waited for Deitz to remember the notorious Mr. Hatfield, whose public relations firm had recently been all over the news due to a tasteless stunt he'd inadvertently gotten himself entangled in. It only took a few seconds for Deitz to remember the name. When his gaze widened, I nodded. "I see you've heard of him."

"Who hasn't heard of Zeke Hatfield?"

Probably somebody. But around Ashville, the man was famous. Or infamous. "Do you remember his latest escapade?"

"Ah," Deitz said, nodding in understanding. "That was quite a photo."

Deitz was referring to the picture of Patrice and Zeke in a romantic clutch, semi-dressed, in the Pastor's office of Ashville's largest Lutheran church. Being caught in flagrante delicto was only part of the problem. The bigger problem was the fact that it was during a funeral for a popular and very wealthy local stockbroker, with whom Zeke had been doing business. The public fallout for the act had been wide and deep.

"But why would Zeke blame Patrice for that?" Eddie asked. "It sounds to me like they were both at fault."

"Ah, such naivete," I said with a smile. "Clearly, you don't understand the depths and lengths of Patrice's scheming. You see, Patrice has been trying to create a rep for herself as something of a bad girl, fast and loose, to catch the eye of a Hollywood producer looking for fresh talent for a very partic-ular role in his next film. Patrice fit the physical requirements for the role to a tee. But she had what she considered to be the stench of the small town on her. She was looking to make a splash."

"If she was responsible for them getting caught, she certainly accomplished that," Eddie said.

"She did," I agreed. "And poor Zeke lost a million-dollar client over it."

"Okay, that's definitely motive."

I nodded in agreement. "So I propose we start with those three."

Before Eddie could respond, my phone rang. I looked at the ID on the screen and groaned.

"Who is it?" Eddie asked.

I showed him the screen, and he paled. "Don't answer it."

"I have to," I said, a whine in my voice. "He'll just keep calling and then show up here if I don't." Sighing, I answered the call. "Hey," I said to the Lieutenant. "What's up?"

"That's what I want you to tell me," my father said, sounding vastly unhappy. "Come over to the house, Maybell. And bring that worthless PI with you."

I didn't bother asking him how he knew Deitz was there. The Lieutenant was omnipotent in all things having to do with his children.

With a long-suffering sigh, I promised we'd be right over and got off the phone. I looked at Deitz. "We've been summoned."

To his credit, Deitz didn't make a run for it. He simply nodded and asked, "You don't by any chance have a bullet-proof vest I can borrow, do you?"

"Sure. It's pink, says *Punkin* on the back, and is a size small."

"I'll take it."

I laughed. "You'll look good in pink. But the vest won't do you any good."

He frowned. "Why not?"

"Because the Lieutenant would shoot you between the eyes before you could finish saying hello."

───────

The familiar scents of Lavender potpourri and lemon dusting spray greeted me as I came through the door. The worn but comfortable furniture was still arranged the way it had been when I was a kid, and the fireplace danced with soft light despite the heat outside. The Lieutenant liked to sit in front of the fire, so he cranked the air conditioner to accommodate his guilty pleasure.

He wasn't sitting in his usual chair in front of the fire when we came into the house. But I could hear him moving around in the kitchen, dishes clanking together as he unloaded the dishwasher.

"Dad," I called out. "We're here."

Deitz stood in front of the fire, his expression contemplative. The golden light of the flames bathed his handsome face, highlighting the strong chin and furrowed brow.

The Pomeranian Devil shot off toward the kitchen, tail eagerly wagging as he anticipated a reunion with his favorite human tyrant.

The Lieutenant's deep voice easily cut the distance between the rooms. "Hello, rodent," he said, his tone filled with humor and a fondness he probably thought we couldn't hear. "How's my little canine twister today?"

I pressed my lips together to keep from smiling. The Lieutenant wouldn't be pleased if he saw me grinning over his sappy love for my little dog.

Heavy footsteps moved toward us across the scarred, wooden floor. A beat later, the Lieutenant appeared in the archway from the hall, his gruff but still handsome face carefully formed into a scowl.

Shakes bounced in at his side, dark eyes bright and tail whipping happily behind him.

Deitz looked up and blanched when he saw my dad's full attention locked onto him. The fire in the Lieutenant's brown gaze burned hotter than the one on the hearth.

Very slowly, one of the Lieutenant's shaggy brows lifted.

Deitz flinched and moved away from the flames, allowing my dad to lower himself into his favorite recliner in front of the fire.

Shakes wasted no time leaping into the Lieutenant's lap.

I sat down across from them on the comfortable but well-worn couch my mother had picked out when I was five years old. The Lieutenant hadn't changed a single thing in the house since my mother died of cancer more than three years earlier. "What's up?" I asked my dad, keeping Deitz in my peripheral vision as the Lieutenant started scratching Shakes' ears. My pampered little pooch's eyes went slitty with pleasure.

"Sit," the Lieutenant barked at Deitz.

For just a beat, I thought Eddie was going to refuse the command, but he seemed to think better of antagonizing the Lieutenant and sat.

"Tell me what happened at the theatre."

I told him the same story I'd already told Argh. Twice. I should just record the event and play it back to the members of my family. I was pretty sure I'd be repeating it again once my other siblings got wind of my predicament.

When I was finished, silence filled the room, punctuated only by the snap and crackle of an energetic blaze. Finally, the Lieutenant turned a glare on Deitz. "Why were you there?"

"Patrice Reynolds is...was...my client. She'd called and asked me to escort her home."

"Why did the victim think she needed an escort?"

"She was certain she was being stalked by a rabid fan," Deitz said, frowning. He'd spoken with certitude, but something in his eyes told me he was beginning to rethink it.

"Was that a normal part of your job for the victim?"

Deitz stared at the Lieutenant as if he'd suddenly realized my dad had an ulterior motive for his questions. Finally, he said. "No. She initially hired me to find the stalker and get enough evidence to put him behind bars. Recently she'd wanted more protection. If you don't mind my asking, why are you interested in my agreement with a client, Lieutenant Ferth?"

"We'll get to that," dad responded dismissively. "Have you figured out who was stalking the victim?"

"Not yet." If Deitz hated being interrogated, he didn't show it. "She didn't have much to go on. She'd gotten a couple of texts, which were apparently sent from a dumb phone and couldn't be traced back to anyone. She also swore someone had broken into her home a few times, moved some things around, but didn't take anything or leave behind any evidence of a break-in."

"She never saw anyone?" the Lieutenant asked.

Deitz shook his head. "Not really. She'd mentioned feeling like she was being watched and, she swore that she saw a dark-haired man following her through Asheville Mall, though she couldn't really describe him to me."

"Did you believe she was being stalked?"

Deitz hesitated, his expression unreadable. Finally, he said, "It was my job to believe her."

The Lieutenant stared at him a moment longer, derision clear on his stern features, and then turned to me. "Who might have wanted the victim dead?"

I took him through my reasoning from earlier and gave him the three potentials Deitz and I had isolated.

He listened intently and then stared thoughtfully into the fire for a long moment. Finally, he settled his gaze on me. "I agree with your top three potentials. Look into them first." He turned to Deitz. "Your stalker is the prime suspect. Find him."

Then he asked, "May, I don't need to tell you to be careful, do I?"

I sat in stunned silence, too shocked to speak. Finally, I just shook my head.

To Deitz, he said, "Consider me the lead on this particular investigation. You're working for me. Keep me apprised. Let me know if you bump up against legal roadblocks, and I'll try to get rid of them for you."

Deitz was taking the Lieutenant's unexpected support much better than I was. "Yes, sir."

The Lieutenant nodded, his shaggy brows lowering as his hard gaze filled with worry. "I don't like it, May. I'm sure that doesn't surprise you. But my hands are tied here. Your brother's hands are tied. You look good for this murder, and the higher-ups are going to be watching us carefully to make sure we don't interfere."

"But..."

He held up a hand. "I can't let you get railroaded. I won't do anything illegal. But I can do a little behind-the-scenes cover and support action. You two proved yourselves capable of good investigative work before. I'm asking you to do it again."

"Okay," I said after an uncomfortable beat. It was a weak response, but a better one evaded me.

Deitz and I didn't speak again until we were back in Betty, heading to my place. He stared straight ahead, the rain-speckled windshield fracturing the light from oncoming headlamps and animating his unmoving features.

I let him brood for a few minutes, but I needed to talk. The Lieutenant's request had sent my safe, sane little domain into chaos. In a normal situation, the Lieutenant tried to keep me from doing things like investigating murders. In the real world, I found ways around his restrictions. In my reality, the Lieutenant meant well but was overprotective.

But he'd thrown me a curve. He was asking me to do the thing he always told me to avoid. And the reason for the change was nothing short of terrifying.

I'd become a murder suspect, or...a person of interest in a murder.

My freedom was at stake. My life. The thought twisted like a blade in my chest, causing my pulse to skyrocket. It finally registered how much trouble I could be in.

The fear must have shown on my face because Deitz reached across the car and squeezed my hand. "We'll find the real killer, May. It's going to be all right."

I nodded, but his assurance didn't quite ring true. Deitz was scared too. And his fear was like an adrenaline shot to my system. "It's just that..."

"I know," Deitz said. "It's a bit disconcerting having the Lieutenant on our side for once."

"It is."

"But he'll be an asset we didn't have the last time we worked together. And we managed to solve that mystery." He sounded as if he was trying to convince himself. Not me.

I nodded again, my throat dry enough to choke me if I tried to talk.

We fell into uneasy silence again. Around us, the traffic thinned as evening turned to night. Unlike downtown Ashville, the quiet little suburb of Hillside where I lived tended to tug on its PJs and close down for the night by ten pm. I usually found pleasure in the quiet streets. But the soft patter of cold rain made the night suddenly feel lonely.

The relatively empty streets should have made it easier for us to spot the tail. Or notice the moment the dark car behind us started following too closely. I blame our distracted thoughts for the fact that we didn't see the big vehicle surging forward, engine revving.

Until it was too late to escape.

5

The impact knocked my head into the back of my seat and sent my little car shooting forward, out of control. I overreacted, jerking the wheel to the right just as the sedan slammed into us again.

An alarmed yelp from the back seat had me half-turning. "Shakes!"

"I've got him!" Deitz yelled. "Drive."

The car hit us again.

My head banged sideways, connecting painfully with the window. The world in front of my eyes turned muzzy and gray. I was only vaguely aware of the steering wheel spinning out of my grip.

Eddie reached across the car and grabbed the wheel a beat before we smashed into a streetlight pole, giving it a yank.

As the muzziness cleared, I stomped my foot on

the brake and retook the wheel, managing to keep Betty on the road.

Betty rocked to a stop, leaving rubber in a dual trail across the asphalt, and I dropped my head forward with a groan.

Eddie shoved Shakes into my arms. "Stay here!" he yelled as he threw himself out of the car.

The Pomeranian Devil licked frantically at my throat, whining.

"I'm okay, buddy," I lied. "It's okay."

Eddie ran toward the car idling in the street, its darkened interior obscuring the driver. When he pulled the gun he'd concealed inside a waistband holster, the sedan took off with a squeal of tires, nearly clipping him as it hightailed it down the street.

I fought my seatbelt until it released. Betty's door creaked loudly when I shoved it open, and I groaned, clutching my aching head at the sound. Eddie was talking to someone as he strode toward me...probably the police.

I scooped up my dog.

Realization hit me, and my head shot up. I yelped in pain before shuffling toward Deitz. "No, Deitz!" I waved my arms to catch his attention.

"Got it. Thanks."

"You didn't call 911, did you?"

He hurried over, took a squirming Shakes from my arms, and urged me back to the car, easing me into the passenger seat. "I called your dad. He's running down the car's license plate. And he wants you to see his doc."

"The doctor's office is long closed," I argued, resting my throbbing head back on the seat.

Eddie jogged around the car and climbed behind the wheel. To my great pride, Betty started right up. "He says Doc Bathred will be in his office by the time we get there. What kind of power does the Lieutenant have over this guy, anyway?"

My eyes closed, I settled Shakes into my lap, enduring the frantic licking that soothed the little dog. "They were Marines together. They go way back."

"Ah. Leave no man behind. Got it."

"How bad is she?" I asked Deitz a minute later.

My eyes were still closed, but I heard his clothing rustle when he turned to me. "What?"

"Betty. How much damage did she take?"

"Her backside is pretty banged up."

I grimaced.

"Have some faith, May. Argh can pound out the dents. You of all people should know that Betty's best feature is what's under her hood, not the junk in her trunk."

I grinned, offering him a fist to bump without opening my eyes or lifting my head. "Truth."

As promised, Doc Bathred was indeed in his office. The building where his practice was located was a single story that contained a dozen ground floor offices and shared a parking lot with a popular shopping center.

The space was clean and suitable but not fussy. Just what one would expect from the doc's office.

A bell jingled cheerfully as I opened the front door and called out to him. Since it was nearing midnight, the waiting area at the front was unsurprisingly empty of people, including the receptionist, Mrs. Laurell, a no-nonsense woman with a face like a hammerhead shark.

"Doc?"

A door opened down a short hallway, and a square, bristly head stuck out into the hall. "Back here, MB."

Deitz frowned. "MB?"

I shrugged. "Military guys are more comfortable in a world of acronyms. He's called me that since I was a baby."

Deitz snickered. "I'll wait out here?"

"Yep." The last thing I needed was for Doc to think Deitz and I were a couple. The very last thing.

"Who's the boyfriend?" Doc Bathred asked when I walked into his office.

I sighed. "He's not my boyfriend."

"Mm, hm." He pointed toward the chair facing

his desk. "Your dad told me you were dating a PI. That's not him?"

Dangit! My dad and his friends gossiped like old ladies. No, scratch that. No old lady I knew could hope to reach their advanced level of rumor-mongering. "We're not dating," I said a bit defensively. "We just work together sometimes."

Doc dropped onto a rolling stool in front of me. "Uh, huh. Look into this light. Any tenderness or pain?" He shined a pen light into my eyes and had me shift my gaze a few times.

"My head hurts a little."

He shook his head. "Just a little, huh?" He lifted my chin with a gentle finger. "You're too much like your old man. LT could lose a limb and he'd tell me it was just a scratch." He turned off the light and rolled away to chatting distance. "You have a slight concussion. From the description of the accident, you're lucky." I nodded. I didn't ask him who'd told him about the accident. The Lieutenant would have gotten every single minute detail from Deitz and passed it on to his friend.

Doc rolled over to his desk and grabbed a prescription pad, scribbling some stuff on its surface. From where I sat, the writing was pretty much illegible.

"That's not necessary," I told him.

"Mm, hm." He handed me the script, eyeing me

critically. "You getting enough sleep, MB? You look tired."

"I'm..."

"Fine. I know." He gave a long-suffering sigh. "I don't know why I bother."

I chewed the inside of my lip. "Thanks for coming out at this hour to look at me."

He folded biceps like twin roller coasters and narrowed navy blue eyes at me. His craggy face had a few more lines in it than the last time I'd seen him. But he was still a good-looking man for his age. "So, is he an actor too?"

"What?"

He jerked his head in the direction of the waiting room. "The boyfriend."

I decided surrender was my wisest course of action. I'd cede ground to the enemy force, a.k.a. the gossiping band of aging guerillas, and make my escape. "He's not an actor."

The navy blue eyes narrowed further. "He doesn't look like an actor."

"That's because he isn't. He's a PI." I narrowed my baby blues right back at him. "What do you know about actors anyway?"

He shrugged. "I know some actors."

"Mm, hm. Who?"

"You."

I lifted my brows.

"And one other patient."

"You're making that up."

"Nope. In fact, I think you might be interested in talking to this actor patient of mine."

"Really? Why?"

"Because I believe he's dating the victim whose murder you're investigating."

I blinked in surprise. Apparently, the band of aging guerillas did more than gossip. "Dad told you about our investigation?"

"He did. When he told me who the victim was, I recalled one of my patients talking about his girl-friend, the actress." Doc sat back, his expression turning thoughtful. "Thing is, I got the impression this guy didn't think all that much of your victim. In fact, if I was a shrink instead of a GP, I'd diagnose him with serious unresolved issues where Patrice Reynolds was involved."

I sat forward in my chair. "You don't say."

"I did say," he responded, frowning. "But that's all I *can* legally say. Patient doctor privilege and all."

"Mm, hm."

"Before you go, though." Doc grabbed something off his desk, handing it to me. I looked down at a small plastic card and frowned. "Why are you giving me a loyalty card from a warehouse store?"

"Oh," Doc said. "That isn't yours? I thought you'd dropped it."

I looked at the name on the card. Bradley

Cooper. I let a smile curve my lips. "Nope, see, this says it belongs to Bradley Cooper."

"My bad." Doc took the card back from me. "It seems Mr. Cooper must have dropped it when he was in here yesterday. It was just lying on the floor where anybody could have seen it. People are always dropping things around the front desk when they dig for their insurance cards." He slipped the card back into his pocket. "I'll mail it back to him."

"I don't suppose you'd let me return it to him personally," I asked, still grinning.

"Get out of here," he said gruffly, his wide mouth twitching with humor.

I stood, clutching the script he'd given me as I bent to kiss him on a bristly cheek. "Thanks, Doc. I owe ya one."

He called after me as I left his office. "Just take your medicine, and we'll be even."

"Uh, huh," I responded noncommittally.

6

I leaned my head against the window, my eyes heavy. After visiting Doc Bathred the night before, Deitz had driven me home and parked poor Betty until Argh had time to look her over. My brother had called me early. Too early, given that I'd barely been asleep for a couple of hours when the phone rang.

"The car that ran you off the road was stolen. The plate Deitz gave us led me to a ninety-year-old woman, who looked confused. Apparently, her son had taken the car and keys away a year ago, when she came home from a trip to church with corn stalks sticking out of her grill."

I winced. "I don't suppose she was a Wiccan, communing with the natural earth?"

Argh snorted out a laugh. "Nope. And there was likely a very unhappy farmer somewhere between her house and the church. The woman sent me to her son, and he insists the car had been in his garage the night before. But, he'd helpfully left the keys in the ignition because a buddy of his was coming to take it into the shop and tune it up in preparation for selling it."

"Did you check out the buddy?" I asked.

Argh's hesitation told me he didn't appreciate me questioning his prowess as a cop. "No, May. I thought I'd just let that slide. I'm not feeling very curious at the moment."

I stuck my tongue out at him. It was a wasted gesture since he couldn't see through the phone. "Dead end?"

"Yeah. The buddy checked out. He'd gotten busy and hadn't had a chance to fetch the car yet."

"So it looks like it really was stolen."

"Yep. I'm digging into that today. But I wanted to let you know we don't have the guy in hand yet. Be careful out there."

Three hours later, Deitz and I were heading to our first potential killer interview. Both my eyes and my brain were blurry from lack of sleep.

Or maybe the slight concussion was making me sloggy. I wasn't sure. One thing I *was* sure about was that my muzzy brain wasn't being caused by the meds Doc Bathred prescribed for me. Since I'd never filled the script.

Oscar Miller lived in a sprawling contemporary

ranch in the eclectic suburb of West Ashville. A hip and trendy enclave, West Ashville was known for its upscale shops and eateries offering up organic fare. It was the perfect spot for a rising thespian, and I had no doubt Oscar Miller's dramatic genius would be appropriately appreciated and nurtured there.

Miller's home was a masterpiece of clean lines, pale-gray brick, and glass. The carefully manicured lawn featured a pleasant mix of Mountain Laurel, pine, and hickory trees, as well as lowbush blue-berries.

The drive had no gate, which surprised me a little, but I suspected Miller's non-traditional child-hood probably gave him a more egalitarian view-point that might not be at home in the wealthier areas of the city.

Eddie parked his truck behind a low-slung sports car painted a subdued and classy black. We climbed out to the sound of barking from inside the home.

"Sounds like he has a fluffy little fiend of his own," Deitz said teasingly.

I snorted. Judging by the bellowing barks coming from the home, Miller's little fluffball could prob-ably bench-press Shakes with three paws tied behind its back.

Not that my little Pomeranian Devil wouldn't hold his own in the end. I had complete faith in the Pom. Also, there was the elephant and the mouse theory of battle. Shakes thought he was the elephant, of course, even if he was actually the mouse.

Deitz rang the bell and the barking surged closer, along with the thump, thump, thumping of really big paws.

Something massive and black slammed against the long window at the side of the door. Despite having known it was coming, I jumped and took two steps back. An enormous face smashed against the glass, smearing it with copious amounts of slobber. Large white teeth clanked against the slimy window.

"Back, Sampson," a male voice said, just before a disembodied hand appeared in the glass and tugged on the Great Dane's spike-laden collar. Between the name and the collar, Oscar Miller was swimming in a pool of cliches.

Not that the dog wasn't big enough for his name or worthy of the collar. I was sure he was more than worthy of both.

The door opened a crack amid enthusiastic whining sounds. Miller stuck his head out, his body jerking as if his "fluffball" was putting him through his paces. "Can I help you?"

"Oscar Miller?" Deitz asked.

"Yeah. Look, if you're selling something, I'm kind of busy right now." As if to prove his point, he was suddenly jerked back into the entry amid a cacophony of clicking nails. He reappeared with a sheepish grin. "Sorry. He's a puppy and overly enthusiastic."

I forced my mouth not to fall open. "A puppy? How big will he get?"

Miller winced. "Not much taller. But he'll probably get a lot wider and heavier. I'm in a race to get him trained before he gets big enough to drag me around the neighborhood at the end of his leash."

I grinned. "Good luck with that."

Miller's light green gaze sparkled with good humor. "Yeah. But I wasn't lying about being busy. We were in the middle of a training session. Heaven knows we need it."

"It's about Patrice Reynolds," Deitz said, holding up his credentials.

Miller paled, his lips tightening. "I'm sorry about what happened to her. But if you're here to accuse me of killing her..."

I shook my head. "We're just trying to find a killer. To do that, we need to know as much about her life and relationships as possible. Can you spare a few minutes to help?"

His hesitation told me more than anything how mad he was at Patrice. He must really believe she'd stabbed him in the back.

"Please, Mr. Miller," Eddie said. "It would be a huge help."

Miller sighed. "Five minutes." He closed the door

in our faces. A minute later, he reappeared, coming outside to join us. "Let's do this in the back."

We followed a trail of large, natural pavers around the house to a small garden with a waterfall pond and a round wrought-iron table with four chairs.

"Please sit." As we sat, Miller glanced at his watch, leading me to believe he was serious about the five minutes.

Apparently, Eddie noticed too because he got right down to business. "Mr. Miller, when was the last time you spoke to Patrice?"

Miller didn't hesitate. "Last week. And it was the actual last time. I wanted nothing more to do with her. Ever."

"Because you believed she leaked the hit piece in the Asheville Theatre News?" I asked.

He shook his head. "I don't believe it. I *know* it. She all but admitted it to me."

"Why would she do that?" Eddie asked. "You were an important member of the project she was directing."

"You're being way too rational," Miller said, frowning. "Patrice didn't have a logical bone in her body. She was emotionally driven. I'd hurt her ego, so she lashed out. It's as simple and idiotic as that."

"She wanted you to sleep with her?"

I winced at Eddie's directness, but I respected it

too. If Miller was only going to give us five minutes, we didn't have time to dither.

"Yes." Miller's answer was unequivocal. "Even if she hadn't tried to force me onto the casting couch, I'd have never seen Patrice romantically. She was a blight on the theatre world. A diva with no talent to back up her massive ego. I wish I knew who she'd slept with or threatened to get the job of theatre director in the first place."

"Strong words," Deitz said. "You sound mad enough to have killed her."

Miller's frown deepened into a glare. "I told you, I didn't kill her."

"Why should we believe you?" I asked, my tone gentle.

He slid his glare to me and held my gaze for a long moment before looking away, his expression softening. "I was mad, yes. But I've been dealing with people like Patrice Reynolds all my life. Bullies. Narcissistic monsters. Self-involved to a criminal level. The only way I'd survived in the system as a kid was to lock my emotions away. If having someone stab me in the back for not bowing to their wishes was going to make me a killer, there'd already be a long line of bodies in my background."

Deitz tilted his head. "Are there?"

Miller blinked in surprise and then gave a harsh laugh. "No, Mr. Deitz. There are no bodies. I killed them with kindness instead. It's my trademark move, haven't you heard?"

"Suppressing anger is unhealthy," Deitz said. "At some point, it explodes into rage at the very least, and, potentially, violence. Maybe Patrice Reynolds was the unfortunate recipient of that explosion."

Miller sighed, reaching into his pocket to pull out a small lined pad. Catching me staring at the pad, he explained. "I jot down perceptions and observations for my roles." He looked at Deitz. "Do you have a pen?"

"I have one," I said, digging into my oversized bag and finding a pen at the very bottom, beneath random makeup items, hand lotion, sanitizer, gum, a wad of clean tissues, and a book I'd been trying to read for weeks.

Miller took the pen and jotted down a phone number. He handed it to Deitz. "That's Sampson's trainer. We were in a private class at his compound last night." Miller stood up, leaving the pen on the table. "Please don't come back unless you have a warrant."

"Wait!" I said, standing up too. "If you didn't kill Patrice, do you have any ideas who might have wanted her dead?"

Miller stared back at me for a beat, his expression unreadable. Finally, he inclined his head. "The answer to that is easy, Ms. Ferth. Anybody who's ever spent more than five minutes with her."

I watched him walk away and wished I'd done a better job of asking questions. But then, it probably wouldn't have made any difference.

Oscar Miller might not have killed Patrice Reynolds, but he didn't much seem to care who did it either. Which made me wonder. Was he protecting the real killer?

I stood and went after him. "Why won't you help us?" I asked Miller as he started around the corner of the house. To my surprise, he stopped, turning startling green eyes framed with dense blond lashes to me.

"Ms. Ferth, do you consider yourself a good judge of character?"

I frowned, biting back an immediate response. As an actress, I prided myself on my observational skills. I cataloged mannerisms and emotions to use in my craft. But did that mean I was good at judging peoples' hearts? "I'm not sure," I finally responded honestly.

He gave me a tight smile. "You're honest. I appreciate that. As you probably know, I grew up mostly on the streets. In that environment, you learn to read people because it's dangerous...sometimes deadly... not to. I knew from the moment I met Patrice Reynolds that she was trouble. She was the type of woman who'd do or say anything to get what she wanted. And to make things worse, she was very insecure. That insecurity often drove her to lash out at others." His gaze narrowed slightly. "Some people don't appreciate being belittled and threatened."

"It sounds like you're thinking of someone in particular," Deitz said.

I hadn't felt him join me. I'd been too tuned into the magnetic personality across the patio.

Miller shrugged. "That's my point, Mr. Deitz. There isn't any one person you can pinpoint whom Patrice annoyed and threatened. There really are too many suspects to count." He gave us a sad smile. "I feel for you two. I really do. Isolating Patrice's murderer from within the hordes of people who wished for her demise is going to be like plucking a single brown hair from a grizzly's back. Lethal and impossible."

And with that, Oscar Miller stepped around the house and disappeared from sight.

Deitz and I shared a look. I sighed. "Let's go talk to the next person on my short list."

7

Unfortunately, neither Jenna Plum nor Zeke Hatfield was available to chat. Jenna's assistant explained that her boss was getting a massage and had threatened the poor woman with the loss of her job if she interrupted.

Zeke wasn't at his home when we arrived.

"How'd you get his address and phone number, anyway?" I asked Deitz.

He winked. "Trade secret."

I thought of Bradley Cooper and smiled. "Good. I'll let you apply that trade to getting an address for Bradley Cooper, the victim's unhappy boyfriend."

"Consider it done."

We were in Deitz's truck, driving toward home, and my mind was racing. "This isn't going to be easy, is it?" I asked, rubbing my tired eyes.

"I could channel my Nana Horbuckle and say that nothing worthwhile ever is."

I grinned his way. "Nana Horbuckle? That isn't a real name."

"That's the name I always knew her by."

"I hope she lived up to it," I teased.

"Nana Horbuckle was a wise woman who kept Papa H. on his toes for their entire sixty years of marriage." He looked at me, his expression earnest. "I used to think she was a witch. She knew everything I did almost before I did it. Now, looking back, I realize I was just not as sneaky as I thought I was."

Laughing, I said, "Maybe channeling Nana is a good idea. She could tell us who killed Patrice."

"Nah, her powers only worked on her grandkids."

I shifted in my seat and my pocket crinkled, reminding me of the dog trainer whose number Miller had given us. I extracted the small piece of paper. On a whim, I dialed the number, showing it to Deitz when he sent me a quizzical look.

"Loudan Training and Kennels, how can I help you?" The speaker was a woman rather than the male voice I'd been expecting. "Hi. I'm looking for Lincoln Loudan."

"Is this about a training issue?"

"No," I said. "We wanted to ask Mr. Loudan a couple of questions about one of his clients."

There was the briefest pause. "I'm sorry, Mr.

Loudan won't speak to you about one of his clients. Have a nice day."

I opened my mouth to argue and was met with silence. "She hung up!"

"What did she say?"

"That Loudan won't talk to me about another client."

Deitz pulled into the lot at my apartment and parked, frowning thoughtfully. A moment later, he opened his door and glanced my way. "I have an idea."

I winced. Four more terrifying words had never been spoken.

A bell over the door jangled in warning as we stepped into the bright and orderly storefront for Loudan Training and Kennels. The place looked like an expensive pet boutique. The back wall was bathed in soft pink velvet, falling in drapes that held photos of perfectly groomed dogs and happy fur families. Floating shelves contained a careful selection of canned foods, grooming supplies, and bakery-style pet treats. A rack of designer dog fashions ran the length of one wall. Near the front door was a sitting area with two comfy chairs and a small round table. A kitschy table lamp, whose base was shaped like an elegant wolfhound, sent a soft golden glow into the room.

The desk table in the center of the space was kidney-shaped, with pink velvet pillows along the front edge where customers could settle their little darlings while they paid for their purchases. The room smelled like lavender and vanilla.

In honor of the occasion, I'd dressed Shakes in his best navy, burgundy, and forest green argyle sweater and brushed his soft gray coat into a fluffy cloud. His tail curled high and proud behind him, and his black button eyes sparkled with excitement. He pranced toward the woman sitting behind the desk table and looked down his tiny nose at her as if to say, "I, the prince of all canines, have arrived. You may ply me with food."

No dog lover was immune to Shakes. As expected, the woman was totally charmed by my darling little devil. She beamed down at him. "And who do we have here?"

I gave her my best, proud mama smile and jangled the jewel-studded bracelets on my wrist. Like Shakes' leash and collar, they were covered in cubic zirconia rather than real diamonds, but she didn't need to know that. All I had to do was sell it.

It was a role I was enthusiastic about portraying.

The door jangled again and Deitz came inside, holding a small brown bag out in front of him and wrinkling his nose with disgust. "He piddled and doinked on the sidewalk, MayBell," Deitz told me in a very good imitation of an indignant rich guy. "It was quite embarrassing."

I flipped a dismissive hand in his direction, then covered my nose. "Why on earth did you bring it in here? Shakespeare's going to swoon with horror at the stench."

The woman came out from behind her desk, dark brown eyes gleaming. She was no doubt assessing potential sales in her mind as she watched our little show.

"Yip!" Shakes bounced off the floor as the woman approached and pranced over to sniff her shoe.

She laughed, giving him a fond look that I was pretty sure she was faking. "He smells my little Pom Penelope." Giving me her best faux-sincere smile, she gushed, "I just love the breed, don't you?"

Sorry sister, I thought. *I know acting when I see it, and yours isn't even good enough for a high school production.*

Somewhere in the distance, a cacophony of barking reminded me that the place was much more than just an upscale pet supply store with a faker for a clerk. I glanced in the direction of the noise and pinpointed the door that no doubt led back to the kennels.

The woman noticed me noticing the noise and made a sound of disgust. "I'm sorry about that. It's close to dinner time, I'm afraid. What can I help you with today?"

"For starters, you can take this for me," Deitz said, grimacing.

The woman's friendly expression died on the vine. Nope, not an animal lover at all. "Of course." She grasped it with the very tips of her perfect fingernails and walked toward the back door with it at the end of her extended arm. She quickly opened the door a crack and flung the bag through without looking where it went.

Barking exploded through the opening and was muted again when she shut the door.

Her smile looked a little worse for the wear. "Now, what can we do for you?"

I looked down at my dog. "It's Shakes. I'm afraid we're having the devil of a time getting him to eat his food. I buy the most expensive food I can find, but he still sticks his little nose up at it. My friend Glynn told me her prize bulldog, Elvis, used to snub his food when he was depressed."

We all scanned our gazes toward the floor, where an obviously not-depressed Shakes wagged and winked.

"Yes, he does look distressed, doesn't he?" the woman asked.

I nodded in agreement, allowing lines to form between my brows. "I'm just about at my wits end. I was hoping Mr. Loudan could help my little darling."

The woman's eyes lit with dollar signs. "Oh, yes. I'm sure he'd be pleased to help." She walked around the desk and opened a shallow drawer in the center, extracting a form and a pen from its depths. "If you'll just follow me, we'll get you all set up and see if Mr. Loudan has time to give you a quick assessment."

The office where she stashed us smelled pleasantly of lemon dusting spray and freshly brewed coffee.

The furnishings consisted of a large oak desk with a black leather chair and two comfortable armchairs covered in charcoal gray fabric.

The wood floor shone with a walnut finish that didn't look as if it had ever been touched by a dog's nails. A small dog bed, shaped like an adorable burgundy velvet couch, sat beneath a large window. Shakes made a beeline for the sofa as soon as we entered the room. He'd been happily perched there looking like the royalty he believed himself to be since the door closed behind the unpleasant clerk.

The back wall of the place sported two book-shelves which, upon my closer inspection, contained dozens of new copies of training books written by Loudan.

"I didn't know he was an author," I muttered as I flipped through one of the books.

Deitz ignored me in favor of snooping through every drawer in the place.

Loudan kept us waiting for nearly thirty minutes. While we waited, Deitz picked through the contents of the desk drawers, and I skimmed through the leather-bound appointment book sitting on top. We quickly discovered the office was a well-appointed fake. Loudan didn't keep anything interesting or important in it.

After that, we sat in the armchairs and waited, sipping steaming cups of coffee we'd made with the single-serving pod brewer in the corner.

The door behind the desk finally opened and a man came through, his bright green gaze sliding directly toward me. Our clerk must have filled him in on who the weak link in the duo was.

I smiled as he shot toward me like a cubic zirconia-seeking missile. "Hello, hello," he said, his gaze sliding toward the book I still held. It was the one on feeding a healthy pet, and I'd purposely held onto it in preparation for his arrival. "I see you've been looking through my books. They're twenty percent off for my clients."

Lincoln Loudan reminded me a little bit of a Christmas Elf. He was probably two inches shorter than my own five feet nine inches, with longish prematurely-gray hair, a bulbous nose, and two rosy spots on his plump cheeks. His eyes were bright blue and his ears stuck out from his head.

Loudan wore chocolate-brown slacks and a dress shirt with the sleeves rolled up, showing off surprisingly strong forearms. The cream-colored sweater vest made him look older than what I guessed was probably mid-fifties. The laugh lines at the corners of his eyes told me he smiled a lot. But after meeting his insincere store clerk, I wondered if his smiles were even real.

Loudan took the hand I offered him between both of his warm, calloused hands. "Ms. Ferth. It's so nice to meet you." He ignored Deitz completely, but that was all right. Deitz was most likely watching the man like a hawk, picking up subtle clues about his personality that we could use to our advantage when we got down to our real business there. "Mr. Loudan. Thank you so much for seeing us on such short notice. I know you're very busy."

He shook his head, flipping a dismissive hand. "It's my pleasure." He nodded toward the book I still held. "That was my most interesting work. I'm fascinated by the way nutrition affects our furry friends." He finally tore his gaze from me and looked down at Shakes, who'd bounded over at the first sign of a fresh victim. "What a cute little fella," Loudan said. He crouched down and offered Shakes his knuckles to sniff. "His eyes are bright. His coat looks healthy." He watched Shakes move for a moment and then straightened. "I see no ill effects from his eating habits. He's maybe a bit thin. That wouldn't overly concern me unless he was a senior. But your paperwork said he was four?"

I nodded. "His birthday was last week." That was the truth. Deitz had told me to stick to the truth as much as possible so we'd have less chance of getting tripped up. We'd celebrated with peanut butter spread on thin slices of apple. Shakes and I had both enjoyed the treat.

"Well, then. We won't worry about his weight as long as he doesn't lose any more." Loudan cocked his head. "You believe he's depressed?"

I nodded. "I just don't know why else he'd suddenly become persnickety."

He held his hands out in a grabbing motion. "May I?"

I nodded.

Loudan gently plucked Shakes off the floor and settled him on top of the desk, running his hands over the Pom's tiny form and checking his teeth. "He's a marvelously healthy little fella," Loudan finally pronounced with a grin. He settled Shakes back onto the floor and sat on the corner of his desk, looking thoughtful. "Does he ever eat non-food items? Or chew excessively?"

Forgetting for a moment that I was acting a part,

I blew a raspberry. "He eats anything and everything that passes under his tiny nose."

Loudan nodded. "Any vomiting? Diarrhea?"

I was starting to forget why we'd come. Lincoln Loudan really seemed interested in helping us with our fictitious problem. Despite myself, I was starting to like the man. "He vomits occasionally. No diarrhea. But when he has to go, he really has to go." I thought about our occasional mad rushes outside.

Loudan nodded. "It's possible his strange chewing habits are giving him a tummy ache. I see this all the time with intelligent dogs. Your little fella is suffering from an ailment that we can definitely work to correct."

I found myself leaning forward in my chair in anticipation. "What is it?"

Loudan's elfish face lit up in a grin. "He's bored."

I blinked at him for a minute and then frowned. "Bored?"

He nodded. "It's really not uncommon for dogs with a keen intelligence."

"Is there something we can do to help him?" I asked, sliding a worried glance toward Shakes.

Behind me, Deitz cleared his throat, then pretended to be looking at the books when Loudan and I both looked his way.

Message received. "If you can help my little guy, I'd be very grateful."

Loudan beamed at me. "Absolutely. We can train

him on food-motivated puzzles and coping mechanisms. My success rate for this particular problem is very good."

"When can we start?" I asked, letting my eyes sparkle with excitement.

"It happens that I have a new Coping class starting tomorrow. Is two o'clock in the afternoon good for you?"

Deitz cleared his throat again. I shaped my expression into a frown. "Oh, darn. I can't do afternoons. Do you have any evening classes?"

"Not during the week," he told me, looking disappointed.

"How about a private lesson?" Deitz asked, striding over to join us. "Would you give a private training session at night?"

Loudan shook his head. "No. I'm sorry. I start my day very early. I'm not much good to anybody after about five pm."

Deitz and I shared a look. Deitz gave me a slight nod. He turned to Loudan. "Mr. Loudan, we're investigating the murder of Patrice Reynolds."

Loudan blinked. "The actress?"

"Actor," I said automatically. "You don't call a female police officer a copess or officeress, do you?" Loudan just blinked at me. I shrugged off my oversharing. It was a pet peeve of mine.

"One of the people we interviewed told us he and his dog were here last night."

"Who was it?" Loudan asked.

"Oscar Miller."

Loudan sighed. "He did actually stop by last night, around six-thirty. I stayed here so I could give him the natural calming chews I'd ordered for Sampson."

"Was he here long?" Deitz asked.

Loudan glared at Eddie. "You came in here under false pretenses and wasted my time." He turned his glare to me. "That was very unprofessional of you."

I winced, feeling guilty. "It wasn't totally a lie. I actually think you can help Shakes."

Loudan lifted a hand and shook his head. "Please leave before I call the police."

I bit back a response, knowing it wouldn't go well for anyone if I told him to call the Lieutenant.

"We haven't done anything illegal." Deitz pulled out his credentials. "And, as far as wasting your time, if you'd just answer our question, we'll get out of your hair."

I dug around in my purse while Loudan and Deitz had a glare-fest.

Finally, Loudan sighed. "He was here about fifteen minutes. Now please leave."

I stood, clipped Shakes' leash on his collar, and placed a wrinkled twenty on the desk. "I *am* sorry. I'd like to buy this book. Thank you for your time." I could feel Loudan's speculative gaze on me as I strode out of the room. But I didn't look back. I couldn't shake the feeling that there was more to the strange little man who seemed to genuinely love dogs than he let anyone see.

Would he lie to protect a killer? Or to frame an innocent man? It was something Deitz and I would have to figure out. But I realized, as we sailed past the unlikeable woman in the shop, that I really hoped Lincoln Loudan was exactly what he appeared to be.

8

"What now?" I asked Deitz.

He'd been quiet during the drive across town...thoughtful. He pulled himself out of his thoughts at my question, shaking his head. "We're blocked on the other two suspects you laid out. At least until tomorrow. But we have the boyfriend."

"The boyfriend," I said, nodding. "Bradley Cooper."

"Yeah," Deitz said. "I ran a quick background on him while we were waiting for Loudan. He's an interesting character. He works for the city as a building inspector. From everything I've found, he has an acerbic temperament. He's hacked off a lot of the commercial building contractors in Ashville."

Curled happily in my lap, Shakes' small body twitched from a dream. I smiled at how cute he looked. "That sounds promising," I said. "Do we know where to find him?"

Deitz nodded. "He lives a few miles from here. I have his address."

"Let's go then."

Bradley Cooper lived on a quiet residential street that backed up to a much dicier part of Ashville. Clinging to the city's skirts, Cooper's street still held a smidgeon of its original charm, though the nineteen fifties style homes were definitely showing their age.

Still, Cooper's home showed signs of having undergone some level of renovation. The brick had been painted a glossy cream color, and shutters had been added to the windows, the wood stained rather than painted. A new roof and a stamped concrete sidewalk gave the place a fresh look that stood out from most of the other homes on the street.

Deitz pulled up to the curb and stopped, eyeing the pair of legs sticking out from under a classic Ford truck. His eyes caressed the truck's pleasing curves and pristine bumpers, and I thought I heard a soft sigh.

"Nineteen fifty-seven model F-100," I said, awe in my voice. "Argh would pee himself if he saw it."

Eddie threw me a look filled with surprise. "You know your classics."

I shrugged. "I have two brothers. But, I'll admit, I didn't really pay attention to their car lust until I got

Betty and realized the magic in a gracefully aged car."

He nodded.

Betty had been Argh's car from senior year in high school. He'd put all his time and money into restoring her powerful engine, doing only minimal work on her untidy little body. He enjoyed watching people underestimate her prowess, often gleefully leaving them in her dust when they least expected it.

I'd caught the same fever and cherished every ding...every treated rust spot. The old car was more than a collection of metal parts to me. She was a symbol of how people could be deceived by appearances. As a woman with blue eyes, delicate features, and long, red-blonde hair, I'd been underestimated all my life. Like Betty, I liked to think I had more going on under my hood than people seemed to think.

Eddie's gaze warmed, something sparking in its depths. "Has anybody told you that girls who like cars are very sexy?"

I climbed out of his truck, leaving an unhappy Shakes behind. "You're an idiot, Deitz."

Trying to ignore the way his deep chuckle made something in my belly warm and tighten, I slammed the door and headed for the legs protruding from under the truck. Despite my desire to focus on Mr. Cooper and his relationship with Patrice, I found myself reaching out to run my fingers over the hood of the classic vehicle, admiring the truck's nostalgic lines and perfect finish. It had clearly been repainted, Ford hadn't offered a bright blue paint in the fifties, but everything else had been lovingly restored to keep the truck's original identity pure, from the distinctive bumper to the Ford lettering on the tailgate.

A chorus of unhappy yips from behind me ensured that the man under the truck couldn't have missed our arrival.

"You like?" the aforementioned man asked.

I looked down just in time to see the rest of Bradley Cooper emerge from under the truck. He pushed off the mechanic's creeper and stood, rubbing his hands on an oily rag. His smile was slightly predatory, but not in a scary way. More like a man flirting with a woman he'd just met.

I nodded. "It's a beauty. Did you restore it yourself?"

Cooper nodded. "It's a hobby."

"I'd love to know how to do this," Deitz said, stopping beside me.

Cooper blinked as if he hadn't noticed Deitz until that moment. "Yeah. My old man used to work at a body shop. He taught me the tricks." Cooper frowned. "Is there something I can help you with?"

"Yes," I told him, smiling to soften what I was about to say. "We need to know about your relationship with Patrice Reynolds."

"Patrice?" Cooper grimaced. "What evil is that woman up to now?" He shook his head, kicking the creeper lightly with the toe of his sneaker. "I swear, if I'd known what a shrew she was, I'd have never gone out with her."

I frowned at him, my opinion of his character sliding down the scale a few notches. "You know she's dead, right?"

Cooper stilled, his expression tightening. "Dead?" His wide shoulders drooped slightly and he seemed to fall against the truck, leaning on it with his hip. "It can't be. I just talked to her..." He trailed off, his gaze skimming to us with a guilty edge. "I didn't kill her if that's why you're here."

"We're not accusing you of anything," Deitz told the man. "We're just gathering information at this point. We were hoping you could shine some light on Patrice's last days."

Cooper shoved the oily rag into his jeans pocket. "I'm sorry to disappoint. I hadn't seen Patrice for a week. She and I broke up."

"Do you mind my asking why?" I asked.

He frowned, his gaze lost in the distance. It took him so long to respond, I thought he was going to refuse to answer my question. Finally, he sighed. "I guess it doesn't matter anymore." His gaze finally slid to mine. "She hit me up for money. A lot of money."

"Did she tell you what she needed it for?" Deitz asked.

Cooper shook his head. "No. But when I declined, she tried to threaten me, accusing me of taking bribes from contractors." His glower darkened. "I told her we were through. She didn't take it well."

"What do you mean?"

He settled a hostile gaze on me, giving a sour laugh. "If you used your imagination, you could probably figure that out all by yourself."

His condescending tone, the way he leaned closer, using body language in an attempt to intimidate me, told me we weren't dealing with a nice guy. I felt Eddie moving up behind me, his heat comforting at my back, but I knew I couldn't let Cooper bully me. So, I clamped down on a niggle of fear and leaned just the tiniest bit closer to him. The Lieutenant hadn't raised a shrinking violet. "Humor me."

His lips tightened into a thin line, his jaw flexing with tension. Finally, he laughed, the sound tight. "I got myself into a little bit of trouble a couple of years ago. It wasn't a big deal. Just a few fists thrown in the heat of anger. The other guy gave as good as he got, and we ended up shaking hands." He shrugged. "But if my employer found out about it, I would have been fired. I can't afford to lose my job."

"Who'd you pick a fight with?" Deitz asked.

"That isn't important," Cooper said. "Patrice threatened to tell my boss about the incident."

"That sounds like motive for murder," Eddie said.

Cooper snorted. "With Patrice, it was just a Tuesday. She gave me reasons to throttle her on a daily basis."

I stiffened at his casual mention of violence. "Did you?" I asked.

Cooper slid his gaze back to me, something empty behind their glossy brown surface. "Did I what?"

"Did you throttle Patrice? Were you aggressive with her on a regular basis?"

Cooper scrubbed a hand over his grease-speckled jaw. "That's none of your business."

I let my eyes go wide. "Maybe not. But I'm pretty sure the police would like to know about it, considering Patrice was murdered."

Cooper blinked in surprise. "Murdered?" He shook his head as he seemed to realize how much trouble he might be in. "I never touched her in anger. She liked it a little rough sometimes, that's all."

"How rough?" Eddie asked.

Cooper's expression shut down. He jerked his head toward Eddie's truck. "I'm done talkin' to you two. It's time for you to climb back into that truck and take that yippy rat out of here. His constant yapping is giving me a headache."

Realizing we weren't getting any more out of Bradley Cooper, we left.

As soon as we were back in the truck, Eddie said. "I'll dig around and find his last employer. If we discover that fight had anything to do with a woman, I'm putting Bradley Cooper at the top of our suspect list."

Shakes growled softly, his body rigid as he stared toward Cooper until we turned the corner.

"Shakes agrees," I said, frowning. I hadn't liked Cooper either. But the fact that he was a jerk didn't mean he was guilty of killing Patrice. "I wonder what she needed money for." I looked at Deitz. "Do you know if Argh found a phone at the scene?"

"I have no idea. But I know who would."

I winced. Despite his insistence that I keep him apprised, I really hadn't planned to call the Lieutenant. "Okay, I'll call my dad. But I'm hungry. Let's head to my house, and I'll make us some sandwiches."

"**D**ude!"

I let go of Shakes' leash and let him run to Doug. Beside me, Eddie tensed as if he thought my neighbor's greeting presaged bad news.

"Hey, Doug. What's up?"

Straightening up with Shakes clutched in his arms, Doug threw Eddie a glare. "Still can't shake the cockroach, eh?"

Deitz blinked in surprise. "You spoke an entire sentence."

Doug's smile was secretive. "'Course."

I opened the door to my apartment and called for Shakes. Eddie came inside and Shakes followed...pulling an amiable dread-head in his wake. I spun around, shocked. To my knowledge, Doug had never come into my apartment. We'd held many an abbreviated conversation in the hallway. And I'd once ventured into his apartment while he'd retrieved a package that had been delivered to his apartment by mistake.

It had been a memorable experience. I'd stumbled back out a few minutes later with a second-hand high, vowing never to set foot in there again.

I blinked at my neighbor. "Oh. Good," I said awkwardly. "You came for a visit. Would you like a sandwich?"

Doug settled Shakes to the floor and gave me wide eyes, which was probably supposed to communicate something, but it only looked like he had a gas bubble to me.

"Is that a yes?" I asked.

My neighbor nodded.

"Is meatball okay?"

"That sounds delicious," Eddie said, eyeing Doug.

A man of few words, Doug gave me a thumbs up.

I headed for the kitchen, wondering what fresh nightmare Doug was cooking up in his smoke-addled brain. As I sliced chicken meatballs in half into a casserole dish and poured spaghetti sauce over them, I listened to the two men talking in my living room. To my surprise, Doug actually contributed some words to the conversation.

I'd have loved to know what they were talking about.

I spread olive oil on ciabatta bread and toasted the bread halves while the meatballs heated in the microwave. Layering slices of Provolone cheese onto each half, I added the meatballs. Settling the sandwiches onto plates, I added a handful of chips and put the finished product on the table. "Lunch," I called out, hearing Shakes' little claws clicking across the tiles as I pulled bottles of water out for each of us.

"That smells delicious," Eddie said.

We shared a smile. "Thanks."

Doug dropped into a chair, snapped his paper napkin on the air to open it, and jammed it into the round neckline of his tee-shirt. He was taking a bite before Eddie and I even sat down. He closed his eyes and moaned with appreciation. "Delicious."

I suddenly wondered if Doug ever ate real food. He rarely left his apartment, and the one time I'd been in there, bags of chips and empty pizza boxes had been strewn everywhere. "Thanks," I said again.

"No, really. This is the best sandwich I've ever had," he said, giving me an earnest look.

I pressed my lips together to keep from smiling. "That's probably just your medicine talking."

"He chuckled. No, man. My cannabis is medical grade. It doesn't give me the munchies."

Eddie grinned at me.

We ate in silence that was only interrupted by the sound of crunching chips. Eddie and I watched with amusement as Doug moaned and swayed and generally acted out his pleasure with the meal. When he'd swallowed his last bite, my neighbor settled his slightly blurry gaze on me. "I didn't want to interrupt while you were eating."

Eddie's smile slid away. "I knew it. Something happened, didn't it?"

Doug frowned at Deitz.

Throwing up his hands, Eddie stood and collected the plates. "I'll stay out of it."

"What's up?" I asked my neighbor. "Did Pinella trot down the hall in her underwear again?" I asked, waggling my brows.

Pinella Gerrard was an octogenarian spinster

down the hall from us who thought she was a sexpot. She also thought Doug was a hottie and had a tendency to trot down the hallway with a measuring cup to knock on his door. She was usually wearing a robe that gaped disturbingly to highlight her matching granny panties and bra.

Doug had stopped opening the door to give her sugar. She was probably swimming in the stuff. Instead, he hid behind his peep hole and waited her out. He'd told me the last time that Pinella wanted a type of sugar from him that he wasn't willing to give.

Doug didn't laugh at my teasing about Pinella. "Worse."

That had my eyes widening. "What could be worse than an eighty-year-old woman asking you for sugar?"

Deitz snorted.

"Be serious, May. This is bad," Doug scolded.

I straightened my spine. "Okay. What happened?"

"When I came home from buying groceries today, there was a guy skulking around Betty."

Eddie stopped smiling. "What did he look like?"

"I don't know. He was wearing a hoodie. When he saw me coming, he started running down the street like he was just out for a jog."

Eddie relaxed. "Maybe he was. He might be a classic car enthusiast who just wanted to check Betty out."

I nodded. "Betty's very interesting."

Eddie lifted his brows like he wasn't sure if I was pulling his leg.

I grinned. "As you know, I like when people underestimate her."

He shook his head. "What about the guy's build? How tall was he? Slender? Beefy? Young or old?"

Doug thought about it for a minute. "Maybe close to six feet? He was a little too meaty to sell the jogger routine."

"Meaty as in overweight or musclebound?" I asked.

"It was hard to tell in the loose sweats and hoodie, but I got the impression of softness rather than muscle."

"Okay, so heavyset and slightly over average height. Did he move like a younger man?"

Doug nodded. "Thirties, maybe."

"Thanks," I told Doug, giving him a smile. "That helps a lot."

He nodded and headed for the door. "I'll keep my eyes open." He stopped with his hand on the door handle. "I won't let anything happen to you, May."

He gave me a puppy-dog look that sent alarm bells clanging inside my head. What was going on?

My phone rang as Doug closed the door behind him. I glanced at the screen, wincing. "It's the Lieutenant."

9

"Punkin, I need to see you. I'll meet you in fifteen minutes at Ashfield Park. Usual spot." In typical Lieutenant fashion, he disconnected without giving me a chance to respond.

I pulled the phone away from my ear and stared at it, my mouth hanging unattractively open.

"What is it?" Deitz asked. "What did he say?"

"He said he needs to see me in fifteen minutes," I told Eddie. I grabbed my purse and slung it across my body, calling for Shakes. The sound of his tiny nails clicked toward us down the hallway.

Eddie pulled his keys from his pocket, but I shook my head. "We don't need the truck."

"Okay," Deitz said, frowning. "Is he picking us up?"

I attached Shakes' leash as he vibrated with excitement.

"There is no 'us.' He said he wanted to see *me*. Not both of us." I headed toward the door, moving fast. The park was a fifteen-minute walk once I got outside. I'd be late unless I jogged part of it. The thought made me grimace. The sandwich and chips were sitting in my belly like twin lead balloons.

"I'm not letting you go alone, May," Eddie argued as I shooed him out and locked the door behind him. "Not after what Doug just told us."

I rounded on him, poking a finger into his chest. "Don't tell the Lieutenant about that, Deitz. I mean it."

A sly look crossed his handsome face. Alarm bells chimed in my brain. Eddie said, "I won't tell him. Unless you refuse to let me come to this meeting."

I glared at him. He lifted midnight brows and crossed his arms over his chest.

I blew out a frustrated sigh, spinning to hurry toward the steps. "You need to keep up. The Lieutenant gets cranky when I'm late."

"Ugh!" I said when I spotted the large, pacing form of my dad. I turned to Deitz and punched him on the arm.

"Ow! What was that for?"

"It's your fault I'm late."

"No. It's your tyrant of a father's fault. He should have given you more time."

"The Lieutenant isn't about fair or not fair. This was a test, and I failed it."

"Just blame me," Deitz said, blinking in surprise when I met my dad's glower and said, "It's Deitz's fault," even before the words finished leaving Eddie's mouth.

The Lieutenant turned a terrifying look on Eddie. "I don't believe I included you in the invitation."

Eddie snorted. "Invitation? From where I stood, you barked an unreasonable order and May had to hop to or risk a dressing down from you."

The Lieutenant nodded. "Well, at least you understand something."

Somebody growled. I didn't think it was me. "What did you want to talk about?" I asked the Lieutenant after flinging Deitz a warning glance.

Scouring Eddie with another glare, the Lieutenant refocused all his attention on me. "I need an update."

My stomach twisted with alarm. "What's happened?"

"MayBell..."

I shook my head, holding up a hand to stop him. I might dance to his drummer in an attempt to keep the peace, but I was nobody's sock puppet. Every once in a while, it was important to remind him of that. "Tell me. Has something opened up in the Patrice Reynolds investigation?"

The Lieutenant held my gaze, a muscle ticking in his formidable jaw. I refused to look away, knowing that if I did, he'd claim the win and refuse to tell me anything. Finally, he sighed. "Your brother found a notation on the victim's calendar that would seem to implicate you."

Ice slid down my spine. "What did it say?"

He shook his head. "That's not impor..."

"Of course, it's important," Eddie interrupted. "May needs to know what she's up against if you want her to defend herself."

The muscle in my dad's jaw ticked faster. But, after a tense moment, he nodded. "MB backstage, seven pm."

"MB? That's it?"

He gave me an exasperated look. "Yes, *MayBell*. MB. Do you know any other MBs on this case?"

I rolled my eyes.

"You are currently the prime suspect in the investigation," he told me. "Having your initials in the victim's calendar for the time she was murdered does not help."

"But I haven't heard a word from Argh," I reasoned.

"Don't let the fact that your brother hasn't interrogated you yet confuse you. He's holding off because I've assured him I have you well in hand."

My eyes went wide. "You told Argh you're helping me?"

"Of course not!" he bellowed. "Do you think I'm an idiot?"

No, I did not think that. My dad was a lot of things. But stupid wasn't one of them. "He's going to be really mad when he finds out."

"You let me worry about that." His words were dismissive, but I didn't miss the regret flickering through his hard brown gaze. "Tell me what you've done so far on the investigation."

Eddie and I outlined our conversation with Oscar Miller and our subsequent visit to Lincoln Loudan's training facility.

"Loudan didn't verify Miller's visit the night before?" the Lieutenant asked.

"He claims he doesn't take evening appointments because he starts his day very early."

"So, Miller was lying," the Lieutenant said.

"Not entirely," Eddie disagreed. "He implied he was there for training with his young Great Dane. Loudan claims Miller only stopped by for fifteen minutes to pick up some chews he'd ordered for them."

"What time does the trainer say he left?"

"Around six forty-five," I told the Lieutenant. "I believed Loudan. He's very odd, but he's almost a dog whisperer. I think he can help Shakes." The words felt familiar as if I was repeating myself. I hadn't even thought Shakes needed help before meeting Loudan. Maybe he was a human whisperer too.

The Lieutenant's gaze narrowed on the Pomeranian Devil. Shakes was sniffing the ground near the merry-go-round, tail wagging. "What's wrong with the rodent?"

Eddie snorted. I threw him a look.

"Nothing. Not really. He just seems stressed."

"Loudan thinks he's bored," Eddie added, lips twitching.

To my surprise, the Lieutenant nodded. "Makes sense. He's very intelligent. Smart dogs get into trouble because they're bored."

I stared at the Lieutenant until he frowned. "What?" he asked.

"Who are you, and what have you done with the Lieutenant?"

Dad rolled his eyes. "Who did you speak to next?"

I filled him in on what Doc Bathred told me and about our subsequent interview with Bradley Cooper.

"He's at the top of my suspect list," Eddie told the Lieutenant.

"Why?" Dad asked.

"He's arrogant, angry, and has at least one episode of unfurling his temper on another human being. But the biggest reason was the way he treated

May. He tried to intimidate her. He treated her like she was weak and stupid."

Dad glanced at me. I nodded. "He did try to treat me like I was nothing. He clearly doesn't respect women, and he specifically doesn't seem to have liked Patrice. I could see him killing her in a fit of rage."

The Lieutenant nodded. "I'll do deep background on him. See what pops up. What's next?"

"We have two other suspects to interview," I told him. "That's our top tier. At that point, we need to look deeper at the people around her. Maybe shift our thoughts on motive."

"Who are the two?"

I quickly went over my reasoning for looking at Jenna Plum and Zeke Hatfield.

The Lieutenant frowned. "You need to tread carefully with Jenna Plum," he told me. "The Plums have enough money to make your lives miserable."

"Understood," I told him. "I don't plan to accuse her of anything directly."

He didn't look happy about my talking to the heiress, but the fact that he didn't try to stop me spoke volumes. He either thought I was in enough trouble to justify it, or he thought she was a viable suspect.

"Don't represent yourselves as working with the police," he warned. "Just tell her you're an old friend of the victim's, and you're looking for information.

It's better she thinks you're just nosy than that you might be investigating."

"Any advice for Zeke Hatfield," Deitz asked.

The Lieutenant frowned. "Guys like that respect only two things...power and money. You two have neither, so he'll probably try to keep from talking to you. You're going to need to sneak up on him."

"Okay," I said. "We should get going. We have lots of work to do."

To my surprise, the Lieutenant pulled me into a hug that nearly broke my ribs. When he pulled back, he looked worried. "Your brother is going to have to bring you in for questioning soon," he told me. "It can't be helped."

"Will he arrest me?" I asked, my stomach twisting.

"Right now, everything he has is circumstantial. But if he finds anything solid..." He shook his head. "I'll let you know what I learn about your suspects. Be careful you two."

———

D eitz left me to run an errand, promising to call if he found a way to speak to our suspects. I settled into the late afternoon sunshine, walking slowly and enjoying the warmth of the sun against my skin.

Shakes bounced happily along, sniffing everything that came within five feet of him and peeing on most of it. I wondered how something so small could wring so much liquid from what had to be a minuscule bladder.

I reached my apartment building and made the turn, heading for the front door. Passing the over-sized oak tree clinging to the edge of the complex's parking lot, I glanced toward the window of my apartment on the third floor, wondering if my suspicious visitor, a.k.a. The Jogger, would return.

Right on cue, I caught movement out of the corner of my eye, and my heart skipped a beat. My footsteps stuttered when I spotted the slender figure cloaked in a black hoodie moving from one tree to the next in the side yard.

I jerked to a stop and dove behind the oak, tugging gently on the leash in my hand. "Shakes!" I panic-whispered. "Come."

My dog bounced over, happy to play whatever game I was initiating. The hooded figure slid from one bush to another near the lower floor windows, his gait strangely familiar. I waited until he'd ducked behind the bush closest to the front door and then I ran, diving behind a large evergreen ten feet away from the building.

The figure's head came up, his face obscured by the soft cloth of the hoodie. But I could tell that he was staring toward the other end of the building, so I took the opportunity to cut the distance between me and the bushes, ducking behind a wood and metal bench when the hoodie swung my way. Tugging Shakes close, I scratched beneath his chin to keep him quiet.

The hooded figure suddenly rose, the faceless hood scanning the grounds as if he'd lost whatever he was looking for.

Shakes fought to escape my grip. I desperately rubbed his belly. He squirmed free and gave me an indignant yip, tail high and swinging to show he was irritated. I made another grab for him, but he skittered away. "No, Shakes!" I'd intended to whisper, but the call came out much louder than I'd planned. I stood up and started after him. "Shakes! Bad boy."

I circled the evergreen looking for my naughty dog, then jolted to a stop when a darkly-clad figure stepped in front of me, face obscured within a black hoodie. I yelped in surprise.

A hand snaked out, wrapped around the back of my neck, and smashed my face into the prickly evergreen. Hot breath bathed the side of my face as the hooded intruder leaned in, his voice like stones against gravel. "This will be your only warning. Stay out of my business or die."

"Hey!"

The figure shoved me hard, and I screamed as I fell into the tree's spiky branches. I fell to my knees wrapped in the tree's prickly embrace. My ears finally registered the sound of Shakes' frantic yipping, which was coming closer with my every raspy breath.

"Dude, that was him!" Doug said as he grabbed hold of my arm and yanked me unceremoniously and painfully free of the tree's grasp.

I stumbled out and caught myself on Doug's sweatshirt-clad shoulder. Peering into his slightly dazed eyes, I clutched the soft cotton beneath my fingers. My neighbor smelled like marijuana and laundry softener. His face was chalky and his eyes were wide. "That was the guy I was telling you about. He was messin' with your car."

"That was you skulking in the bushes?" I accused loudly. I was smack dab in the middle of an adrenaline rush that had me clenching the front of Doug's hoodie and giving him a little shake.

"Dude!" Giving me an indignant glower, he reached up and firmly removed my fists from his shirt, smoothing the crumpled fabric. "I was spying on your stalker. I was tryin' to help."

"Why in the world would you do that?" I asked. "He could have killed you."

"Because Eddie asked me to keep an eye on you," Doug responded, looking hurt. "I could tell that guy was up to no good, so I was keeping an eye on him. And I was right." He pointed a long finger toward the parking lot. "He did something to Betty."

I looked in the direction he was pointing and sucked in a gasp, my hand flying up to cover my mouth. My stalker had done something all right. He'd done something horrible. "Betty," I murmured sadly. Tears filled my eyes as I stumbled toward my poor car.

"...hear me?"

I realized a moment later that Doug had been talking to me, but my mind had gone foggy. All I could see was the butchery...the destruction. All I could hear was the blood roaring through my veins. All I could think was that I was about to be in a world of hurt.

I forced my feet to move around the car and unlock the trunk, dropping my keys to the ground on a quiet intake of breath as I stumbled backward. A brief moment of stunned inaction was all I could allow myself. Then, panting and sweating under a monster adrenaline rush, I choked out, "Doug. Call Argh."

10

I slumped on the front steps, watching the lights on two police cars strobe the area. For the first few minutes, I'd observed Argh interviewing Doug, trying to figure out what he was asking by Doug's reaction.

It had been entertaining but impossible to decipher.

Whatever questions Argh was asking, I was pretty sure Doug wasn't giving him a response that people who weren't medically high could understand. My suspicion was verified when I snuck another look their way and saw the gobsmacked expression on my brother's face.

"May?" My head jerked toward Eddie. He was striding in my direction, worry painting his features. "What's going on?" He swung an arm toward the cluster of trouble in the parking lot.

I deflated, not wanting to explain why I was probably going to prison. "You should stay away from me. Save yourself."

Eddie stared at me for a minute and then sat down on the step, wrapping an arm around my shoulders and tugging me close. "Tell me."

I would have, but then a black Escalade turned into the lot, and suddenly I couldn't breathe. "The Lieutenant," I choked out.

"May, tell me before he comes over."

"I don't have enough time."

"Give me the Internet version, short and fast."

The Lieutenant stepped out of the big car, and his gaze slid unerringly to me. We stared at each other for a minute. Then he gave me the briefest of nods, and I discovered I could breathe again. It was his way of saying he was still on my side.

"May?"

"The quick version is that the guy Doug saw skulking around Betty came back," I told Deitz. "He took a blade to Betty's paint job and then opened her trunk and poured blood in there. If I had to guess, I'd say it was probably Patrice's blood."

Deitz stared at me for a long moment. "Okay."

I expelled a sigh, dropping my head into my hands. "I know. It sounds absolutely crazy. But that's what happened."

"Did anybody else see the vandalism?"

I lifted my head, my expression no doubt rippling with despair. "Just Doug."

Eddie closed his eyes and grunted. "Perfect."

"Yeah. There's still time for you to make a run for it."

He rubbed my arm, dipping his forehead to mine. "I'm not going anywhere. We're going to figure this out."

"Punkin?"

Tears sprang to my eyes when I looked up at the Lieutenant. "I didn't kill her," I said, my voice strangled by tears and emotion.

He inclined his head. "Tell me what happened."

I told him. Eddie didn't speak through the entire unbelievable story. But when I was done, he said, "Her neighbor has seen this guy hanging around Betty before. He's clearly setting her up, sir."

"Neighbor? You're talking about the pothead?"

I groaned softly. No matter what Doug told them. No matter how much detail he managed to wring from his strange brain, nobody was going to give the information any weight. "It's medical-grade, Dad."

The Lieutenant stared at me, one eye twitching. "That might be the case, Punkin. But it's not going to make him any more reliable as a witness."

"So, what now?" I asked.

"Now, I take you to the station. Argh needs to interview you."

"Can't he do that here, sir?" Eddie asked.

I had to hand it to him. Eddie was being as respectful as I'd ever seen him with the Lieutenant. It was strangely concerning. As if he thought I was two small steps away from the electric chair.

"It's best if we make this as official as possible," Dad said. He held my gaze for a long moment, willing me to understand what he was saying. They didn't want to give anybody an excuse to scream favoritism.

I nodded and shoved to my feet, feeling twenty years older than I was. "Let's go."

Eddie stepped between me and the Lieutenant, head high. "Sir, you'll want to interview me too."

A strange smile twitched on my dad's lips. "That was the plan, PI. Follow us in."

"It's the police!" purred a high-pitched, reedy voice from behind me. We all looked up to where Pinella Gerrard stood with one hand holding the front door open. She was arranged suggestively against the frame, one knobby knee cocked in an obvious pose.

"Lord in Heaven," the Lieutenant murmured, his expression turning slack.

Despite my dire circumstances, I felt a grin curving my lips at his reaction.

The eighty-year-old woman was wearing a lacy black peignoir and black feathery slippers with pointed toes and kitten heels. She'd combed her pink, cotton-candy hair straight back into a high ponytail and topped it with a red silk rose. Her pale face was covered in wrinkles, reminding me of a picture I saw once of sand waves in the Mojave desert.

Garish purple eye shadow set the stage for the inch-long fake eyelashes that were so heavy she could barely keep her eyes open.

Lipstick the color of a baboon's behind had been layered onto her thin lips, the color leeching into the vertical wrinkles around her mouth. She was holding her usual prop, a plastic measuring cup that might never have seen so much as a grain of sugar.

Seeing my dad, she batted her lashes hard enough to bruise her cheeks. The spiky things looked like frantic moths trying to escape her face. I worried she'd tip forward from the weight of them and fall down the steps. "Mr. Police Officer..." she murmured huskily. Starting down the steps, Pinella swung her skinny hips as she descended. Every step was accompanied by the wobble of a kitten-heeled slipper, her wrinkled knees quaking under the unnatural hip movement. "I was just going to borrow some sugar, and I saw the lights through the window."

To our collective horror, she batted the moths again. I was struck with an unreasonable need to pluck them off her face and set them free.

Somehow, she managed to spot Deitz from beneath the unwieldy lashes, and her eyes widened in delight. "Oh my, it's a veritable man buffet out here, isn't it?" She winked at me, propelling one moth into a frantic and tawdry dance.

"Hi, Mrs. Gerrard. Are you looking for Doug?" I felt bad throwing poor Doug to the wolves. I really did. But when the force of nature that was the spinster Gerrard was on the hunt, it was every man for himself. "I think he's talking to the officer over there." I pointed vaguely toward the parking lot. "My car was vandalized."

To my surprise, Pinella Gerrard stopped eyeing Deitz long enough to snap a look my way. Her startling turquoise orbs, easily her best trait, widened with surprise. "The young man in the hoodie? I saw him skulking around." She shook her head, setting the I Dream of Jeanie ponytail into a dance. "I knew that boy was trouble."

"You saw the man who vandalized my car?" I asked before the Lieutenant could stop me.

She bobbed her head in the affirmative. "I did. He had a big knife in his hand and was trying to duck behind the car. But I saw his wide backside."

The Lieutenant stepped forward. "Ma'am, why don't you get dressed, and we'll give you a ride to the station so you can make a statement."

Pinella's turquoise gaze widened with affront. She ran a knobby hand down the front of her peignoir. "I *am* dressed, officer." She gave him a smile that no doubt weakened the Lieutenant's bowels. "I'd think a big handsome guy like you would like having a woman in silk and lace on his arm."

The Lieutenant stared at her for a moment, his Adam's apple bobbing. I watched in fascination, having never seen my dad discombobulated about anything. Then he seemed to shake it off. "I'll have someone give you a ride to the station."

With that, he spun on his heel and strode away, looking like he was trying to outrun flames licking at both of his heels.

———

A rgh stared at me across the table. He seemed to be mentally cataloging all the ways I'd screwed up my life and his. I let him do his thing, knowing he'd feel better after he finished lining it all up in his brain.

I leaned my cheek on my fist and sent my wish for a cup of coffee into the universe. Maybe the wish would tickle one of the cops out in the bullpen, and someone would take pity on me.

Argh shifted in his chair, and I knew he was about to hit me with his best stuff. "What part of 'keep your head down and stay out of trouble' did you not understand?"

I didn't bother sitting up. With the pad of my index finger, I traced a heart that had been etched into the table where I sat. "What part of somebody carved the words 'Break a Leg' into my car and poured blood into my trunk do *you* not understand?"

He shook his head, looking utterly disgusted with me. "What did you do to draw that kind of attention to yourself?"

My OCD blazing, probably because it was the only thing I had control of at the moment, I finished tracing the arrow that pierced the carved heart before responding. After letting Argh stew for a beat...just long enough...I straightened in my chair and slid my gaze to the camera in the corner of the room. I skimmed Argh a glance in silent question.

He gave a minute shake of his head.

Okay then. We were being recorded. I couldn't mention Dad. "I've been questioning suspects, trying to find Patrice's real killer."

"What suspects?"

I told him about my top three prospects, as well as the two offshoot interviews we'd done as our pool of potential suspects expanded. When I was done, Argh looked a lot like the Lieutenant had when he'd cast his eyes on Pinella Gerrard.

"You've got some nerve, MayBell," Argh said too softly for the camera in the corner to pick it up.

I lifted my brows, silently reminding him I had the Lieutenant's blessing.

Argh lifted his, telling me the Lieutenant wasn't in charge of the investigation. He was.

I widened my eyes to remind him who had rank.

He narrowed his, telling me to eat dirt and fart dust.

We held a silent stalemate for a moment, and then Argh sighed. He picked up his favorite blue gel pen and poised it over the small, lined notebook he took interview notes in. "Tell me about finding Patrice Reynolds."

"I've told you three times."

"Tell me again."

I formed my expression into one that told him I was going to put worms in his shoes, but he just waited, pen poised. "Fine," I ground out. "I came into the theatre at just before seven pm..."

"Why were you there?"

"To pick up my copy of the script."

"How did you pick that specific time?"

"Patrice's assistant told me that would be the best time."

"That would be Manny Poe?"

"Yes."

Argh nodded for me to go on.

"I'd been told the script would be on the table nearest the door. It's a long folding table where they usually keep coffee and snacks."

Argh jotted. "Who told you where the script would be?"

"Manny."

"Was yours the only one on the table?"

"No. It was full of them when I got there. Each one was marked with an actor's name."

Argh scribbled into his pad, "Go on."

"I grabbed my script and turned to leave, but then I noticed the spotlight."

He somehow resisted ribbing me about it again. "What's the significance of the spotlight?"

"Everybody was supposed to be gone for the day. Manny had asked me to lock up when I left. The spotlight shouldn't have been on."

"Go back for a second. If the place was closed up for the day, how did you get inside?"

I frowned. "The door wasn't locked."

"Should it have been?"

I wanted to do a facepalm. I should have realized something was wrong. "Yes. It should have been locked." I'd expected Manny to be there and let me in.

I sounded so dejected, Argh took pity on me and didn't gloat that I'd missed the clue. "So, you expected it to be locked?"

"Yes. But, I guess I assumed Manny left it open for me." A stupid assumption. Of course he wouldn't have left it open. Unless...

My gaze shot to Argh's. "He knew Patrice was still in there. That's why he didn't lock up for the night. Patrice probably told him she was expecting Eddie, and she'd lock up after he came."

"You're referring to Eddie Deitz?"

"Yes. He was working for her. She apparently had a stalker." I was getting tired of repeating information, but I didn't want to leave anything out since we were being recorded.

Argh made another note. "Go on."

"I walked out to the stage to see if there was anybody there."

"Was there?"

I thought about it for a beat before responding. We'd come to the meat of the matter. If I misspoke, I'd make myself look guiltier. But, if I told the truth and it was supported by Argh's findings, it would corroborate my innocence. "I thought I saw movement at the back of the theatre, but when I focused on the spot, I didn't see anything."

"Go on."

I left the stage, wanting to get home and let Shakes out of the Pom Hilton. He'd been in there a few hours at that point, and he really needed to go.

Argh lifted dark brown brows at my statement. "Does your dog's bathroom habits have anything to do with the murder of Patrice Reynolds?"

I glared at him. I knew the perfect spot to dig up some night crawlers. Argh was terrified of worms. I smiled at the thought.

He must have read his doom in the curve of my lips because he paled slightly, shifting in his chair. "You headed off the stage..." he prompted.

"Yes. Something shifted above my head and I

stopped, startled by the movement. It was a cable. I remember thinking someone must have bumped against it."

"What did you do?"

"I stood really still and quiet, listening."

"Did you hear anything?"

"No. It was quiet. Then someone flicked the switch, shutting off the spotlight on stage. It was pitch black in there for a minute while my eyes tried to adjust. I heard a swishing sound and backed deeper into the curtains at the edge of the stage. I tried to stay quiet, listening for whoever was sneaking around in there with me."

"What happened next?" Argh had stopped writing and was leaning forward as if transfixed by my story. I didn't blame him. The whole thing was the stuff thrillers were made of. I'd be fascinated too if I hadn't been the one smothering in those dusty curtains.

"I heard the clock ticking and was thinking about Patrice playing the crocodile in Peter Pan in high school..."

He gave me a strange look. I shook my head. "Long story. But I must have laughed a little, and then there were footsteps. The curtains were shoved into my face and held around me. I couldn't breathe and I panicked. I fought and struggled and my fist connected with something fleshy but bony at the same time." I looked at Argh. "Now that I think about it, I think it was someone's cheek. I punched my attacker."

"You're sure you didn't hit the corpse?"

I grimaced. I didn't even want to consider that. "I'm pretty sure I nailed the killer because I heard him run away."

"Him? You think it was a man?"

I blinked at him. "I...I'm not sure. I assumed it was a man because he seemed big. But I guess there's no reason to assume that, right? Patrice was stabbed. That's not generally a woman's choice of weapon, but there are always exceptions." Particularly with rage. I knew from listening to the cops in the family talk that an enraged woman would kill in a much more physical, personal way than women normally did.

"What happened then?"

"I untangled myself from the curtains and felt my way to the nearest light switch. When I turned the lights on, I saw her."

"You saw the victim?"

I nodded, shuddering. "I knew as soon as I looked at her that she was dead."

Argh scribbled in his notebook for a few minutes, the only sound in the room the soft scritch of his pen against the paper. While he worked, I thought about what I'd just told him. It had been a good exercise going over it all again with some time between the event and my retelling. It still seemed a bit surreal, but I felt as if I could step back from it a little...see it more clearly.

What I saw in that new light was that I'd fought with Patrice's murderer and, for some reason, I hadn't shared her fate. Why?

If the murderer was the man who'd defaced my car, he clearly thought it made sense to get me thrown into jail. But if he was threatened by me, why not have killed me that night? A knife would have pierced the aged velvet of the curtains. He needn't have unwrapped me from my velvet burrito to kill me.

I wouldn't have been able to stop him.

I wasn't even able to scream.

So why? Unless it was someone who knew me and didn't want to bring Argh's and the Lieutenant's wrath down on them. Or someone who didn't hate me enough to see me dead. I heard Eddie's voice in the hallway outside the door. He was probably heading to the Interview room next to mine.

I shivered violently as an unwelcome thought ran, unbidden, through my mind.

Could it have been Eddie? Could he have arrived before I did and killed Patrice? But why? She was paying him to protect her.

Unless someone offered him more to take her out.

I wanted to tell myself that was crazy. Deitz had shown no tendency toward lethal violence since I'd known him. He hadn't been at my house when Betty was vandalized, but he'd showed up later, after the police arrived. It was possible that he'd donned a hoodie and done the deed himself and then pretended ignorance.

Could Eddie kill me if he thought I was a danger to him?

I didn't want to believe it. But I was the daughter and sister of cops. One thing cops carried around with them at all times was their cynicism. When you've worked with the worst and lowest of humanity for a while, you quickly learn that anyone is capable of doing anything under the right circumstances.

Even murder.

Even of a friend.

Eddie... My heart felt like lead in my chest.

"What happened to your script during the altercation?" Argh asked, his voice piercing my depressing thoughts.

I blinked, lifting my gaze to his. "What?"

"Your script. Did you still have possession of it after the attack?"

I frowned. "I don't think so. I probably dropped it when I was battling the curtains."

Argh sighed. "The crime scene people didn't find it at the scene."

His unspoken message was that the killer must have taken it. But why?

"You can go now. I know you won't listen to me, but you should probably keep your distance from Deitz. You two are just making more trouble for yourselves by investigating this thing."

It took me a beat to realize what he'd said. "What? Aren't you arresting me?"

"There are two witnesses to the fact that there was somebody skulking around your car and likely defacing it. Go home, May. Lock your doors and stay out of trouble. Promise me."

I couldn't promise him that. I had a killer to find before he decided I was worth killing too.

And it looked as if I was going to have to find him myself. I didn't think I could trust my partner to help me.

My partner, Eddie Deitz.

Because he might be more interested in killing me.

11

I hit the button to buzz Manny's apartment, then stepped back out into the early-morning sun and looked around. I hadn't heard from Eddie since the police took me in for questioning the day before. Granted, I'd shut off my phone so he couldn't call. But when I'd turned it back on, there had been no missed calls from him.

Did he believe he'd accomplished his mission by making me a suspect? Would he just slip quietly away to spend his ill-gotten gains, forgetting to call me again for weeks as he'd done before?

With a jolt, I realized what a great dupe I was. I was connected to the police, giving Eddie the perfect access to information with little or no danger to himself.

I shook my head, more to dispel thoughts of Deitz than to deny the possibility. I couldn't deny that, even if he didn't kill Patrice, his association with me made his work as a private investigator much easier. If my suspicions were right, he currently had the Lieutenant and, to a lesser extent, the detective in charge of the Reynolds investigation helping him navigate a safe course. He also had me as an alibi should he need it.

I had another face-palm moment. I was an idiot.

But then, if I really believed Eddie killed Patrice, why hadn't I told Argh that very thing? I'd had plenty of opportunities to do it. I could have called the Lieutenant the night before and shared my concerns about Deitz.

I hadn't.

Did that mean I really didn't believe Eddie was the killer?

In a desperate attempt to purge my mind of its poisonous thoughts, I stabbed the buzzer three more times in quick succession.

No response.

I glanced at my phone and saw that it was eight am. Yeah, it was a little early, but Manny's job with Patrice had him working all kinds of hours. It seemed likely he would be awake.

I lifted my finger again and the door suddenly opened. I stumbled backward, nearly falling off the concrete pad and down the short flight of steps.

A young woman with green hair and earbuds filling her ears hurried out and held the door for me.

I thanked her and went inside. Manny's apartment was on the first floor. I followed the dingy stripe of dirty green carpet down the hallway toward number 124 at the end and jerked to a halt, my pulse spiking.

The door was slightly ajar.

There was a smear of blood on the wall beside it.

I elbowed the door open so as not to leave any prints and stuck my head inside. "Manny?"

Silence met my call.

I stepped inside, uneasiness flaring as I took in the mess in front of me.

Manny could just be a slob, I told myself. What I was seeing might be normal for him. But I doubted it. Every surface in the tiny apartment was covered in discarded clothing, broken dishes, or torn and crumpled papers.

The small desk near the window was a jumble of paper as if someone had opened the dented metal file cabinet behind it and thrown the entire contents around the room. I moved closer and read the printed words across a torn page resting on the back of the couch. With a jolt, I recognized it as part of a page from the charity production.

Seeing those torn pages, I thought about the strange circumstances of the play. Used to eccentric behavior in the theatre world, I hadn't given much thought to the genesis of the production we'd been about to bring to life.

The rumor was that the play had been written by

whoever was bankrolling the production. I'd read the play before agreeing to accept a role, and I'd thought it was very good. However, the circumstances of its creation were all very hush-hush. When I signed up for a role, we didn't even have a final title for the production yet.

Somebody was playing the game in a big way. Secrecy drew interest from people for whom drama was a way of life. Interest translated to money and a future as a playwright.

Unfortunately, the hidden agendas and secrets made it much harder to find a killer.

Paper lay thick on the cushions of the couch. Some of the sheets were partially covered by pillow stuffing. Pulling the sleeve of my tee over my hand, I carefully pushed the paper aside to check out the damage.

Each cushion had been sliced in a large X pattern, its stuffing yanked out and flung around the room.

I stepped back, seeing the broken glass and wood from framed theatre posters that likely had once hung on the screws which were evenly spaced along the walls. The posters themselves were torn and creased. An unnecessary debasing, given that nothing could have been hidden in them.

Somebody had rage issues.

My cell phone rang, and I jumped with a little squeal. Tugging it from my jeans pocket, I looked down to see that it was Eddie. Refusing the call, I slid it back into my pocket. I considered calling Argh or my dad. But before I did that, I'd search the rest of the small place, looking for clues where I could find Manny. If I could find him, he might be able to tell me what was going on. I headed toward the hallway off the living room.

"Why didn't you take my call?"

I yelped, spun on my heel, and nearly toppled over when the back of my shoe connected with a sofa leg.

Eddie stood in the doorway, his phone still in his hand and a frown fixed firmly on his handsome face.

I stared at him, running through my options. I only had two. Tell Eddie about my suspicions, or pretend nothing was wrong. Then a third option presented itself, and I jumped on it. "Sorry. Argh advised me to stay away from you until the investigation was over."

Eddie cocked his head, not looking even a little surprised. "Why?"

Why indeed? I stalled for a minute by carefully stepping over the debris field around me and moving into a clear spot near the kitchen. The fact that it was even further away from Eddie was just a happy coincidence. "He's mad at the Lieutenant for setting us on this investigation and thinks we're just going to make ourselves look more guilty if we keep turning up at all the pertinent places." That was true, if not really the point. Then I had a brilliant thought. "I have a feeling Lincoln Loudan complained about us." It was certainly plausible, given how angry the man had been that we'd lied to him.

I did an internal wince when Eddie's expression softened into something that looked more like hurt than anger. Guilt was acid in my stomach. I hadn't lied...exactly...but I definitely wasn't telling him the truth.

"Okay. Then why are you *here*?" He indicated the room with a sweep of his hand. "You seem to still be investigating." The obvious implication was that I'd decided to ignore one part of Argh's instruction but was sticking to the "avoid Eddie" part.

Since I didn't have a good reason for that, I decided a good offense was in order. "I could ask you the same question," I told him. "Why are you here? And what were you doing calling me from the hallway?"

Unfortunately for me, his explanation made a lot more sense than mine. "I'm here because it occurred to me that Manny might know who Patrice was afraid of. As her assistant, he checks her email and keeps her appointments. He's actually the one who hired me for bodyguard detail."

"Okay."

"And I called you from the hallway because I saw you come into the building, but I was too far away to get your attention. When I saw Manny's door ajar, I was afraid you might be in trouble."

"Oh." I chewed my bottom lip. "Okay."

He narrowed his sexy gaze on me. "Why does your brother want you to stay away from me?" There it was again. That tinge of hurt running through his gaze and coloring his voice.

I shrugged, uncomfortable with the conversation for obvious reasons. "To be honest, he's not sure how involved you are in all this."

My pulse spiked as soon as I said the words. I hadn't meant to blurt that out. But since it was out there, I watched Eddie carefully for his reaction. I wasn't prepared for what came next.

He laughed.

Actually laughed.

I watched as tears streamed from his eyes and wondered if I should give him a brisk slap on the cheek to jar him out of it.

I glowered at him, but he didn't even notice. "What's so funny?" I finally asked.

Eddie shook his head and scraped the back of his hand under his eyes. "You Ferths," he said a little breathlessly.

Then, like a light switch being flipped, his smile disappeared and his expression filled with anger. "You know what, MayBell? I'm out. I've just been trying to help, but it's clear you're never going to forgive me for the sin of not calling you for a few weeks." He nodded, turning toward the door. "I get it. You're the princess, and you're not to be abused or disappointed in any way." He started out the open door and stopped, smacking the frame hard enough to make me flinch. He didn't even look at me when he said, "Someday, you're going to realize it's pretty lonely up in your ivory tower. For your sake, I really hope you don't figure it out too late."

"Eddie!" I yelled, starting toward the door as he left. I wasn't sure what I even intended to do. Try to get him to see my side? That was a losing proposition. How did I get him to understand that he looked like a murderer? It took me until I reached the hallway to stop my forward momentum.

The entrance door slammed behind Deitz, and I watched him stride rigidly away, his shoulders tight and his steps fast. I sagged against the wall and closed my eyes, pain shooting jagged bolts into my twisting belly.

What had I done?

Nothing good was the answer that popped into my mind.

With a shaky sigh, I pulled out my cell and called the Lieutenant.

The apartment was empty. No Manny.

In a strange twist of lies becoming reality, I endured a sharp rebuke, coupled with deep disappointment from my brother for inserting myself into another crime scene. I didn't even try to defend myself. He was right. I was an idiot.

I stood across the hall of the apartment, leaning against the grimy wall and watching Argh and a couple of uniformed cops sift carefully through the mess, dust for prints, and collect potential DNA samples from the living room and kitchen.

They'd found blood.

Argh had said his piece and was studiously ignoring my presence there. I knew I should leave, but something kept me rooted to the spot. I was worried about Manny. And I couldn't help wondering what his disappearance had to do with Patrice's murder.

My cell rang. I briefly considered not answering it but then decided I could use the distraction. Sliding it from the pocket of my jeans, I hit *Answer* without seeing who it was. "Hello?"

"Ms. Ferth?"

"Yes."

"This is Molly. Jenna Plum's assistant," she clarified.

"Ah, yes. Hello, Molly. How are you?" I pushed from the wall and started toward the front door.

Behind me, Argh called my name. I turned and pointed to the phone and kept going, putting distance between my nosy brother and me.

"I'm fine. Thank you for asking. I'm calling because Jenna can fit you into her schedule this morning."

"Wonderful," I said, meaning it. "What time?"

"Can you be here in twenty minutes?"

I could if the universe conspired to help me, which never happened. With traffic, Jenna Plum lived almost thirty minutes from my current location. "I'll see you in twenty minutes," I told the assistant. Then, I disconnected and took off running.

12

J enna Plum lived on the top floor of a contemporary building that featured high-end shopping and posh restaurants on the first two floors and upscale apartment living on the upper five floors.

I walked out of her private elevator and stepped onto a rug that pulled my sneakers down into endless softness, muffling my footsteps until I hit the cool white marble tile of the foyer.

A young woman sitting behind a matching marble desk lifted her head as I approached. She made a point of glancing at a delicate watch that sparked with silver light beneath the caress of the chandelier high above her head.

Despite the obvious censure in her action, she stood and hurried toward me, a wide smile on her pretty round face. "You must be Ms. Ferth," she said, taking my hand in a firm grip and pumping it once. The assistant stood slightly taller than my own five feet nine and carried about twenty extra pounds. She had a swimmer's build, with broad shoulders and narrow hips, and wore most of the excess weight in her middle. The woman's curly brown hair was cut short and bounced when she walked. Her smile sparkled in her blue eyes.

"And you must be Molly Baucht?"

"That's me." She coughed into her hand. "Sorry. Allergies."

"Jenna's waiting for you. I'm afraid she can only spare a few minutes now. She has a very busy schedule."

"I understand. I'm really sorry to be late. The traffic coming into Ashville was horrible."

"The accident at 240 west and 25 north." She nodded, sending the brown curls into motion. "I used to work at Holmes Brothers out that way. There are always crashes there. "No worries. Follow me."

Molly led me to a pair of French doors in the back corner of the room and opened them, sticking her head inside. "MayBell Ferth is here."

"Come!" called a voice that was melodic and deep. It was a voice that was perfectly suited to the theatre, not as a director but as an actress.

I walked through the door and stopped, waiting for the woman across the room to stop typing and look up. When she did, I forgot to speak.

Jenna Plum was a statuesque woman with long arms and large hands. Her features were strong, and her hair was very short, the dark strands not much longer than a man's business cut. She stood up and came around the desk, a smile curving her wide mouth. My first thought was that Jenna looked like a man wearing a woman's clothes. But I knew that wasn't true. I'd seen her from a distance numerous times at theatre and charity events. She'd always been dressed like the wealthy heiress she was, her long face exquisitely made up and her posture tall and proud. But seeing her face to face and up close was an experience.

Her eyes were a hazel color that was mostly green, with copper-colored specks that caught the light as she tilted her head in question.

She offered me her hand and I took it, her hand swallowing mine. "Ms. Plum, it's a pleasure to meet you," I said.

She gave me a smile that told me she was used to my reaction. "The pleasure is mine. I've met your father," she said, her eyes alight. "He's a very impressive man. I understand he's a widower."

Her expression held blatant interest in a way I didn't want to examine too closely. Not about my dad. "Yes. To me, he's mostly just terrifying."

Her laughter was no delicate ringing of bells. It was full and rich...a bawdy celebration of life.

I liked her a lot.

"Please, sit. Tell me what I can do to help."

I sat, intending to get right down to business. "Molly told me you don't have much time."

Jenna waved a dismissive hand. "I can fudge my schedule by a few minutes." She lowered her tall form into a chair across from me, settling her large hands over one knee. The creamy silk of her slacks and matching blouse shimmered in the sunshine bleeding through a window behind her desk.

"I'm sure you're aware that Patrice Reynolds died?"

The copper flecks in Jenna's eyes flared at the mention of her nemesis. Her wide mouth tightened. "I am." The words were spoken in a tight voice, a clear indication of her feelings for the dead woman.

I nodded. "I know you and Patrice weren't close."

Jenna's bark of laughter made me twitch in surprise. "That's a grand understatement. No. The truth is, as I'm sure you already know, I hated the woman with a passion."

"She stole the director's role out from under you," I said, hoping to get her talking, so I didn't have to worry about asking the right questions.

"Like a thief in the night." She settled back into the chair, a Louis XV reproduction with needlepoint mustard upholstery on a walnut frame. I recognized the style because my mother had been fond of French antiques. The home she'd shared with the Lieutenant had several pieces he'd purchased for her over the years as gifts. "To this day, I'm not sure what happened. I'd spoken to the benefactor and thought I had it locked down. I was starting to plan for the production, and then I received a call from Patrice, gleefully informing me she was taking over as director."

"That must have made you angry."

She laughed again, the sound tight with rage. "Angry doesn't begin to describe what I was feeling." She lifted her chin and her face cleared. If the smile she sent my way didn't quite meet her eyes, I didn't hold it against her. Patrice had a way of incurring wrath from everyone she met.

Jenna cocked her head, her startling hazel gaze narrowing with suspicion. "What exactly is your interest in this? Are you working with the police?"

"I am...was...going to be part of the production." I frowned, letting my real disappointment at losing the opportunity shine through. "I've also known Patrice since high school. I'll admit to being curious." My face flushed at the admission.

Jenna's face cleared and she nodded, running a hand over one crossed knee. "I understand wanting to know more. It's perplexing when someone dies so unexpectedly."

"Yes. Do you mind my asking...who made the decision to hire Patrice?"

She stood suddenly, pacing across the room to straighten a large metal figurine of a rearing horse.

The piece looked heavy, but she shifted it with the touch of a few long fingers. My mind pictured Jenna easily overcoming Patrice, who'd been more interested in having glossy hair and pouty lips than developing muscle. She'd had a soft kind of beauty. Against a woman of Jenna's size and strength, Patrice wouldn't have had a chance. "I'm sure you're aware that the benefactor who was bankrolling the production wishes to remain anonymous." She shrugged. "I'd certainly tell you if I could."

I believed her. "Now that Patrice is gone, will you take the director's role?"

She spun on her heel, fixing me with a penetrating look. "I didn't kill her. That's why you're here, isn't it?"

I opened my mouth, but nothing came out.

She flipped a dismissive hand my way. "Don't worry about it. I know I look good for it on paper. But I wouldn't give that shrew the satisfaction of ruining my life."

"Where were you at seven pm three nights ago when Patrice was killed?"

Jenna sighed. "Getting a massage. Here."

When I stared at her, she nodded. "Molly will give you the name of my personal masseuse. Now, if that's all."

I felt as if I should ask more questions, but I was drawing a blank. I really could have used Deitz's interviewing acumen. "Thanks for making time to see me," I said. I started toward the door. Her voice stopped me.

"MayBell?"

I turned back. "Yes?"

"As you well know, that woman was a human wrecking ball her entire life. She hurt people right and left, creating all manner of hard feelings. But if you don't mind my giving you a piece of advice?"

I nodded.

"I know people. I understand what makes them tick. The person who did this wasn't striking back with rage over hurt feelings. This attack ran deeper than that. Patrice struck at someone's heart…or their dreams. Her murder was an act of self-protection. Not anger."

"She struck at *your* dreams," I said before I could stop myself.

"Yes," Jenna said with a tight smile. "She did."

I thought about what Jenna had said as I headed home. Her advice had the flavor of a confession, but my gut told me it wasn't. Despite the fact that Jenna had the means and motive to kill Patrice, I was having trouble seeing her in that light.

I called Jenna's masseuse from the car, and he affirmed her appointment the night Patrice was killed. Unfortunately, I had to take what he told me with a grain of salt. The man was employed by Jenna. He would likely back up her declaration that she was having a massage just to keep his job.

Molly's verification of the scheduled massage was tainted by the same problem.

Still, it was possible they were telling the truth.

My phone rang after I hung up from the masseuse, and I looked at the caller. It was the Lieutenant. "Hey, Dad," I said, turning on my blinker to make the turn onto my street.

"Punkin. Can you come over for dinner? I'm cooking."

"Is the world ending?"

"Har," he said, a smile in his voice. "I cook all the time. Just not for you."

"Harsh," I said, grinning.

"Sorry, I didn't mean that the way it sounded. I'll see you in an hour?"

"Sure, I just need to..." The truck came from nowhere, a flash of black that slammed into Betty like a battering ram and sent her spinning.

Heart pounding with fear, I braced myself and jammed my foot down on the brake, sending the stench of burning rubber into the air as my tires skidded over the asphalt. But it wasn't my brakes that eventually stopped the car.

It was a tree.

The roar of metal against wood ended in a jarring stop that sent pain shearing down my spine. Something punched me in the face, slamming my head back against a headrest that felt like concrete from the impact. With an extended groan, Betty settled down to earth, her bones bent and broken as steam whooshed out of her twisted front hood.

"MayBell!" My dad's voice seemed to come from far away, throbbing with panic. "Punkin, talk to me!"

Confusion turned my thoughts muzzy. I fought the urge to shake it off, knowing the spears jamming into my skull would object in a most painful way if I shook my head. "Dad...I..." My voice was thick, the words oozing slowly from between my lips.

"Punkin, what happened? Talk to me."

"Something hit me." My hand slipped along Betty's upholstery and found the cool rectangle of my phone, half jammed into the crease of the seat. I lifted it to my ear. "A black truck."

Sounds of moving came through the phone, followed by a door opening and slamming closed. "Where are you?"

"I was turning onto my street," I said, my voice fading out from under me. "Almost home..."

A hand slammed into the window near my throbbing head. I jumped, swore softly, and turned. "Help," I said, too softly for anyone to hear. My vision darkened, and I realized my eyes were closed. "Please?" I murmured.

I fought to open my eyes, but the darkness wouldn't give way. I gave up trying to stay awake as weariness dragged at me, and I let myself get pulled away.

13

"I'm not crazy," I told Argh. "It was a black pickup truck." I frowned. "I think it was Eddie Deitz."

"That's ridiculous, May."

I threw up my hands. I'd somehow entered an alternate dimension. Opposite world. Was I unconscious? Maybe I was in a coma from the crash? I must be dreaming if I had to convince my brother that the man he didn't really like anyway might be a bad guy.

No. If I was living in an alternate reality, I was pretty sure my head wouldn't feel like it contained the drumline from my high school alma mater, Hillside High.

And Betty...

Tears filled my eyes. I'd been avoiding the question, but it needed to be asked. Leaning my head back on the headrest, I steeled myself for the truth. "How bad is it?"

Argh didn't need to ask what I meant. He grimaced before he could catch himself.

My stomach twisted with dread. "Just give it to me straight. Rip off that band-aid."

He engaged the blinker and sighed, turning into the parking lot at my apartment. "She's totaled, May. I'm really sorry."

I sagged into my seat with a soft whimper.

Argh flashed me a look. "You okay?"

I gritted my teeth as a wave of anger slammed through me.

"No. I'm not okay, Argh. Eddie Deitz killed my car. And he tried to kill me."

"First of all," he told me in his best mansplaining tone, "Why would Eddie try to kill you? As far as I can tell, the man's crazy about you."

I tried to remember my reasoning for Eddie being the bad guy, but my head hurt too badly. "He drives a black pickup truck."

"So do half the males in North Carolina and some of the females. Try again."

"He worked with Patrice. Maybe she did something to him. Or maybe somebody hired him to kill her for them."

"Now Deitz is in the business of doing wet work for hire?"

I glowered at Argh. "Maybe."

He laughed at me. Laughed. At. Me! "It could happen, Argh."

"In a bad movie, maybe. But I just don't see any reason why Eddie Deitz would want to kill Patrice Reynolds or you."

"Will you look into him?"

Argh didn't respond. In fact, he suddenly seemed overly interested in the parking lot lines.

"Argh?" My eyes went wide. "You already investigated him, didn't you?"

He parked the car in Betty's assigned spot. The lines around his mouth told me he was fighting to keep from defending himself.

"When?"

Argh looked at me, arching one mahogany-colored brow.

"I can't believe it," I told him, huffing angrily.

"And I can't believe you're mad because I investigated your boyfriend when *you* just asked me to investigate your boyfriend."

"It sounded better when it was my idea."

He laughed.

I moved my head too quickly, energizing the drumline that was busily beating my brain. I closed my eyes and rested my forehead against the cool glass.

"Two concussions within a couple of days is not good, May. You should have stayed at the hospital."

"I'll be better off at home."

"Will you take your meds?"

I crossed my fingers where he couldn't see them. "Um. Yes?"

"Let me see your hands."

I held up my hands, fingers newly uncrossed.

"Okay, swear to me that you'll take your meds as prescribed, or I'm taking you right back to the hospital."

"I'm not going back there," I said, shuddering. Memories of watching my mom die a slow death made hospitals feel like one of the lower circles of Hell.

"Fine," he said.

I relaxed.

"You can stay with Dad."

Oh, heck no! "Ease down, Superpatch. I promise. I'll take my meds."

He nodded, a smug look on his stupid face. "You can't be alone. I'll call Sasha."

"No."

"May," he said in a warning tone.

I held up a hand. "She's got too much on her plate right now. She doesn't need to deal with me too."

My older sister and her husband lived over an hour away. She was pregnant and dealing with a raging case of morning, afternoon, and evening sickness while holding down a full-time job as a cop in a picturesque mountain town that had more than its share of crime. Plus, her husband, Barton, had recently taken a new job that kept him on the road ninety percent of the time. She'd sounded tired and stressed the last time I'd spoken to her.

"I have Doug," I told Argh. "He can check on me. It will be fine."

He thought about it, frowning unhappily, but finally nodded. "I'm calling you every hour to make sure you're still alive."

"I promise I'll answer. Unless I'm dead."

"Har," he said, glowering at me.

Climbing slowly out of his sedan, I headed into the building without looking back. Seeing Argh's car where Betty should have been would only set me off again.

Argh overtook me easily since I was walking like a hundred-year-old woman. He held the door for me, and we took the elevator rather than the stairs, a sign of how miserable I was.

I fumbled my key at the door for several seconds.

"Here, let me," Argh said, grabbing the key from me.

I was so tired I didn't even argue.

Shakes was already barking when I stepped into my apartment.

"I'll take the rodent out for his walk," Argh said. "You take your meds and get into bed."

"Thanks," I told him, tears sliding down my cheeks as he patted me gently on the head like a dog.

"I'm happy to be here for you," my brother, the con artist, told me. "Because that means when I'm sick, you'll have to clean my house and bring me food."

"Not a chance," I told him. "I'm not up on my Malaria and Dengue fever shots, and I haven't had a tetanus booster this year."

He snorted. "My place isn't that bad."

"From the perspective of a rat or a cockroach, it's a palace. But from my perspective, you shouldn't just move out. You should douse the whole thing in gasoline and burn it to the ground."

He rubbed his knuckles on my head in retribution.

I swung at him. "Ow!" Then I shuffled down the hall and let Shakes out of the Pom Hilton.

"Don't rush him in his business," I called out to Argh.

"Yeah, yeah," he responded. Then I listened as he talked to Shakes in a voice that was as close to baby talk as Argh would ever get. Like the Lieutenant, Argh liked to pretend he was too manly to be fond of a Pom. And like my dad, he was full of beans. He adored my dog, and the feeling was mutual.

I smiled as I pulled off my shoes and jeans and climbed under the covers. Despite my promise to Argh, I ignored the pain pills the doctor gave me in lieu of some regular old acetaminophen. I didn't even hear Argh and Shakes leave the apartment. I was already asleep.

I dreamed of a shadowy figure running through a theatre. I dreamed of knives and blood and a screaming diva who'd never been as good at playing a role as she'd been playing a corpse. I dreamed of terror-filled moments struggling to breathe, the dusty press of heavy velvet binding me like a giant spider's sticky web.

Angry faces flashed through my mind.

Harsh words filled with hate tortured my thoughts.

A room torn and smashed...the flash of sunlight flaring off a shiny black hood...the throaty roar of an oversized engine...the shriek of metal twisting.

A hand slamming against glass.

A hand...against glass.

I shot upright with a scream on my lips. Pressing my mouth into a tight line, I stopped the scream just before it escaped.

Something moved in the shadows of my bedroom. "May?"

My head snapped around, and the scream I'd vanquished a moment earlier ripped from my lips.

The figure hurried forward, hands outstretched and palms out. "MayBell, it's just me, Eddie."

Shakes hurried into my room and bounded up his doggy stairs to fling himself at me. The little dog climbed into my lap and scoured me with frantic kisses. I pulled him close, staring through his tiny, pointed ears at the intruder in my bedroom. "You scared the beans out of me, Deitz."

His hands were still up as if he expected me to fly from the bed and commence landing blows on his stupid head. "I'm sorry. I guess I wasn't thinking. Argh asked me to keep an eye on you."

"Argh?" I asked. "My brother left you here to watch me while I slept?"

"Not exactly," Eddie said, looking sheepish. "He left me in the kitchen with orders to check on you every hour. I kind of reoriented that instruction to one that made me more comfortable."

"Well, as long as you're comfortable," I said accusingly. I placed my hand over the thudding organ in my chest. Taking deep, slow breaths, I managed to slow my heartbeat into something that wouldn't kill me.

"How are you feeling?"

I cocked a brow at him, noticing as I did that even that small action hurt my head. "I'm fine, Eddie. Don't I look fine?"

He winced as if I'd struck him. "Well. You mostly just look furious."

"Oh?" I said, steam coming from my ears.

"Yeah. Like a bull in a ring." He placed a hand on his own chest, pinching his red tee shirt between two fingers and tugging it away from his body. "I'm sort of regretting wearing this."

I stared at him for a minute and then barked out a laugh, feeling the tension slide away as I lay back on my bed. "I feel like somebody beat me with a baseball bat and then ran over me with their car."

He nodded, sitting back down in the kitchen chair he'd dragged into my room. "You look..."

I gave him "the look," and his hands came up again. "Great. I was going to say you look really good. Stupendous, even. Fantastic. More beautiful than a sunset. More spectacular than the aurora borealis."

I held up a hand to stop him. "Got it. Thanks. As compliments went, that one was really believable."

He gave me a crooked smile. "Thanks. I thought it was some of my better work."

I snorted.

We fell into silence as I remembered how we'd parted ways the last time we'd seen each other. "I'm sorry," I said a minute later. "For what I said before. I didn't really believe you killed Patrice. I mean, I did sort of believe it, but I don't anymore."

"You don't?"

I shook my head.

"Why not?"

"Three things." I held up a finger. "You don't have asthma." I held up a second finger. "Your truck is a Dodge." I held up a third finger. "Your left hand doesn't have a healing slice on the palm." I gave him a smug grin.

Deitz stared at me, looking perplexed. "Um. Okay, I'll bite. Huh?"

My grin cracked wide. "One of the reasons I'm both a good actor and a good faux cop is because I notice things. I pay attention." I grimaced. "Sometimes, the things I notice have to be literally bludgeoned into me, but that's just a little flaw I need to work on."

When he lifted his brows at me, I gave him a dismissive little flip of my hand. "That's not important now. What is important is that the person who killed Patrice started wheezing after he moved the stage curtains around. Those things are really dusty. Thinking back now, I think he had an asthma attack, and that's why he left the theatre without killing me."

"Okay," Eddie said. "And my truck?"

"The truck that rammed into me was a Chevy, not a Dodge. I saw the logo before it hit me."

He shook his head. "It pays to have a girlfriend who knows cars."

I went very still, afraid to move for fear he'd take it back. "Girlfriend?"

"Would you believe it was just a figure of speech?"

"Was it?"

He shrugged, avoiding my gaze. "Sorry. Forget I said that. Unless you want to remember it?" He slid a hopeful glance over me to gauge my reaction.

Fat chance I could forget. But I shoved it away for the time being, holding up my hand and pointing to the palm. "The person who rammed Betty had a slice on his palm." I showed Deitz where it had been on my own hand. "It was about two inches long and looked angry like it was on the verge of getting infected."

"How do you know that?" Deitz asked, his face paler than a moment earlier.

"I saw it. He..." The import of what I was about to say finally hit me. My gaze shot to Deitz's. "He came over after he hit us."

"Us?" Eddie frowned.

"Betty and me."

"Ah. Go on."

"He slammed a hand against the window." Tears warred with a sense of alarm as I remembered.

The tears won out.

Betty was broken beyond repair. The thought made me immeasurably sad.

"May, that's bad," Eddie said. "Was he trying to get to you?"

"I don't know. I passed out."

Eddie stood up and began to pace. "I need to talk to the Lieutenant."

Shakes leaped off my lap and flew down his doggy stairs, shooting toward the front of my apartment just as an all too familiar voice rang out. "Punkin? Are you awake?"

I sniffed, scraping the heels of my hands across my cheeks to dry them. "I am now," I responded.

Heavy footsteps approached down the hall, accompanied by the soft sound of my dad cooing baby talk to Shakes. "I brought you medicine."

"Ugh!" I groaned, my gaze sliding guiltily to the bottle of pain pills on my bedside table.

The Lieutenant's large form filled the doorway to my bedroom. Tucked in my dad's arm, Shakes wagged his entire body with happiness.

The Lieutenant held out a Styrofoam cup with a red plastic straw sticking out of it. "Medicine for the soul?"

I could have hugged him. "Chocolate?"

He looked almost offended. "What else?"

I made grabby fingers in his direction, and he walked the frozen deliciousness over to me. The Lieutenant sat on the end of my bed with Shakes and watched me inhale creamy chocolate goodness.

He looked worried. His next words were proof of it. "Punkin, I want you off the investigation."

14

"What? No!" I said, so alarmed I stopped drinking my shake. "It's too late, anyway. The killer already knows I'm involved."

Deitz jerked a little and then gave me wide eyes. His expression said, "Ixnay on the ordsway."

He was right. I realized, too late, that I'd said the exact wrong thing.

The Lieutenant stood up and started to pace in the same spot Deitz had been pacing before. "We'll put you into a safe house until we catch the guy. It will be fine. Argh and I will take turns bringing you food and stuff to entertain you."

"Dad," I said.

He ignored me. "A small protection team can watch the house 24/7."

"Lieutenant," I tried again.

He whipped around and, for a minute, I thought

he'd heard me. But, alas... "You still have your pink .38, don't you?"

I groaned, wanting to crumple into a puddle on the floor.

"You have a pink gun?" Deitz asked, his eyes alight with humor.

"Kill me now," I groaned. "Dad, I'm not going to a safe house."

He frowned. "Of course you are, Punkin. You're in danger. There's no discussing it. I won't lose you too."

He stopped talking and swallowed hard, his frantic gaze sliding away from me.

And there it was. He'd lost my mom a few years ago. They'd had a love that survived time and space and even death. Her loss had nearly wrecked him. The big strong Lieutenant had melted into a puddle of goo and given up on life for months.

He didn't want to go through that again.

"Dad, you can't treat me like I'm made of glass."

"I can," he responded, his jaw set into bulldog mode. "And I will."

"You don't try to protect Argh, Sasha, and Dash this way."

"They're cops," he said, looking surprised. "They know how to take care of themselves."

"That's insulting on so many levels," I told him. "I went through almost all the same training they did. You made sure of that. You need to stop treating me like I'll break at the first sign of trouble."

"You're not a cop, MayBell. And you're the youngest."

"Dad, I'm thirty-three years old."

He shoved his big hands into the pockets of his uniform slacks. "You're not going to keep investigating this guy, MayBell."

"She has *me*, sir," Deitz said, his voice soft.

When the Lieutenant looked at Eddie like he was considering taking a bite out of him, I opened my mouth to intervene. But Deitz didn't need me to intervene on his behalf.

"Lieutenant, your daughter is smart and terrifyingly capable. You need to give her credit for that."

Dad frowned, his shoulders hunching.

"We make a good investigative team, her and I," Deitz went on. "We won't take any unnecessary risks. I promise."

The Lieutenant stood in rigid silence for so long, I was starting to think he wouldn't respond at all. But finally, he said, "You'll run every move through me before you make it."

Eddie nodded.

"I'm going to put a uniform on your truck," the Lieutenant said as if he expected push back.

Deitz thought about it for a beat and then nodded. "That makes sense."

Dad and I stared at him in shock.

I found my voice first. "We don't need a babysitter."

"That's the way this is going to play out," the Lieutenant said, glowering down at me. "Take it or leave it. But, if you leave it, you're going into a safe house."

I bit back further argument and sighed. "Fine."

Dad nodded. "Good. Now, let's talk about that truck that hit Betty."

A jolt of pain arrowed through my chest at the reminder.

The Lieutenant gave me an apologetic look. "We ran the plate," he said.

"You got the plate?" I asked, excited despite myself. "How?"

"Neighbor on the corner has one of those door-bells with a camera."

"Did it catch the driver?" Eddie asked hopefully.

"There's no clear image. He was dressed in dark clothes and a ball cap. He kept his face averted. But we got enough of a license number to create a list of possibles." The Lieutenant slid a look to me. "One of them is the missing assistant."

"Manny?"

Dad nodded. "We're chasing that angle. Why don't you two interview the next person on your list." When we nodded, he asked. "Who is it?"

"Zeke Hatfield," I told him.

I was pretty sure the Lieutenant's face paled a

couple of shades. Without missing a beat, he turned to Deitz. "Do *not* leave her in a room alone with that guy," dad said.

Deitz caught my eye. "Don't worry, sir. I don't think we'll be going to any funerals."

Despite our good intentions, we didn't quite make it to Zeke Hatfield's house. After the Lieutenant left, I took my pain pills under Deitz's watchful eye, then shambled off to take a long, hot shower. When I emerged a half-hour later, clean and dressed, I discovered that Eddie had made me dinner.

I smiled when I saw my favorite comfort food waiting for me on the kitchen table. "You made me grilled cheese sandwiches and tomato soup." Moisture stung my eyes, and I blamed the tears on the stupid pills he'd made me take.

"How's your head?" Deitz settled a cold bottle of water down next to my food.

Wanting to be cranky about the drugs, I just shrugged. I really didn't want to give him the satisfaction of admitting I felt a lot better.

Deitz sat down across from me, and Shakes parked himself at my feet, his bright, button eyes fixed on the spot where he assumed the plate and bowl were located on the table. He stared with such intensity at the underside of the table that I started to wonder if he had x-ray vision to go along with his other super-canine abilities.

I dug into my food, surprised to find that I was starving. Then I realized I hadn't eaten anything for hours. I dunked a piece of my sandwich into the creamy tomato soup and ate it, closing my eyes as memories flooded me from my childhood.

"That good, huh?" Deitz asked, a smile in his voice.

"So good. Is this soup homemade?"

I opened my eyes to find the smile on his face I'd suspected was there. "It is. My mom's recipe."

The admission caught me off guard. Deitz didn't talk about his family. I'd kind of just assumed he didn't have any. Which only proved the old adage about how stupid assuming was. "Your mom is a good cook?"

"She was. The best."

"Was?" My voice was soft, apologetic. "You lost her?"

"We did."

"I lost my mom to cancer," I admitted, though Deitz already knew about my family. "How did you lose yours?"

Something hard flitted through Deitz's eyes. "She preferred a bottle and the company of a grifter."

I blinked, realizing his story was much different from mine. "I'm sorry. I shouldn't have brought it up." I said, feeling like crawling away with my tail tucked.

He shook his head. "It's only fair that you should know about my family since I know so much about yours." He shrugged. "I just don't like to talk about her. I stupidly still have hurt feelings about it all."

"That's not stupid," I told him. "You lost her. The way you lost her doesn't matter to your heart."

He didn't respond, only sipping his beer. But there was a new tightness around his jaw and an unhappy light in his eyes.

I ate soup and tried not to ask any more questions, although I was brimming with them.

"My dad lives in Indiana. I always thought I'd go back there someday," Deitz shared a minute later.

"Indiana? So that's where your strange accent comes from."

The haunted look receded as he laughed. "I don't have an accent."

"You actually do. The Midwest accent is very distinctive."

He opened his mouth, presumably to argue with me about it, but my cell phone rang. I reached for it, seeing Argh's name on the screen. "Maybe they found Manny," I told Deitz.

"Hey," I said when I answered the call.

"How are you feeling, Tinkerbell?"

"I'm fine, Superpatch. Just a little headache. But it feels better after eating."

"Have you been taking your pain meds?"

"I've already had the Lieutenant all up in my grill. And Deitz. I don't need to hear from you too."

"Deitz is up in your grill?" Argh asked, his voice little more than a growl.

I sighed. "What do you want?"

"Is that any way to talk to your favorite brother?"

A small smile found my lips, but I took care to keep it out of my voice. "If you were truly my favorite, Betty would be as good as new and parked in her assigned spot right now." I knew he'd take the razzing personally. I also knew it was unfair. It certainly had not been his fault Someone t-boned Betty and me. But Argh and I communicated best in the language of cars. We tended to fall back on it during times of stress.

"That's actually one of the reasons I called."

My spine stiffened and my eyes went wide. "You can fix her?"

"Pipe down Shirley Temple. I'm not a magician."

I drooped unhappily. "I know. It's just…"

"Yeah. I get it. But Dad and I have come up with a solution. It might be temporary. It's up to you."

"What is it?"

"You'll see when I stop by in the morning. Okay?"

Knowing Argh, I didn't waste my breath trying to argue. "Okay."

"Also, I wanted to let you know we found the

truck that hit you. It was abandoned down by the lake, half-submerged."

I hit the speaker button so Deitz could hear. "Eddie's on too. Did you find the driver?" I asked, perking up again.

"The truck was empty. But we traced it back to the owner." He let that hang for a beat.

The brief silence told me all I needed to know. "Let me guess. It belonged to Manny?"

"It did. And the fact that it wasn't really hidden very well told me it probably hadn't been him behind the wheel. Somebody wanted us to find it."

"If this guy is keeping to his MO up until now," Eddie said, "he probably stole the car, used it, and then dumped it."

"Yeah, that's what I think too. Anyway. Stick close to home tonight. The Lieutenant told me that you're going to speak to Zeke Hatfield tomorrow. I think that's a good idea. If nothing else, we can scratch him off the list. But don't go anywhere else without talking to Dad or me first."

I made a face at the phone, earning an amused look from Eddie. "As I said, I have enough babysitters. I don't need you bossing me too."

"Too bad," my brother said. "That's never going to stop. "Later."

"Ugh!" I said when the line went dead. "I'm sick of my family!" As soon as the words came out of my mouth, I regretted them. I was sure Eddie was thinking, "At least you have one."

But he read my guilty look and shook his head. "Stop that. Don't feel bad because you have an annoying family. You're not making me sad." He grinned. "Actually, I'm feeling pretty lucky right now."

I chuckled because that was what he wanted me to do. But his eyes still held a hint of the pain he'd revealed to me.

"What do you say we take Shakes for a walk. Then it's back to bed for you. If you want to have the energy to interview suspects tomorrow, you're going to need some rest."

I sighed. "I'm surrounded."

"I know," he said, taking my dishes and rinsing them before putting them into the dishwasher. "It sucks when people care."

Climbing carefully to my feet, I went to put on sneakers and grab Shakes' leash. My little devil danced excitedly around my feet, nearly tripping me several times. Brief bouts of dizziness had me leaning a hand against the wall, and I thought about telling Eddie I was going back to bed. But I didn't want him thinking I was delicate and sidelining me for the next day's work. So I resolved to take it easy and keep my mouth shut.

Best laid plans and all that.

The night was cool, a soft breeze carrying the scent of roses from the bushes lining one end of the building. We stepped out into a mist so fine it hung in the air rather than falling to the ground in drops.

The sky was the color of lead, only a thin sliver of moon showing through a dense bank of constantly moving clouds. The rain made the asphalt glisten under the parking lot lights and glossed the cars in the parking lot.

Eddie held Shakes' leash. He'd plucked it from my fingers after my little devil had nearly tripped me on the steps.

We walked across the silvered surface of the wet lawn in silence, letting Shakes direct our steps. I pulled long draughts of air into my lungs, enjoying the flowers and the earthy smell driven upward by the rain.

Slowly, all the tension that had turned my muscles to iron and exacerbated my headaches began to lessen as we walked.

"Better?" Eddie asked.

I turned to him and nodded. "Thanks for driving the Pomeranian Devil bus for me."

He laughed. "He's more manic than usual tonight."

"Manic is his specialty."

Silence fell between us again. The rain stopped as we hit the sidewalk. A horn honked in the distance, followed by the squeal of tires. I momentarily tensed at the sounds, memories of the accident crashing over me again.

Eddie dropped an arm around my shoulders and gave me a squeeze. "We'll catch this guy, May. He doesn't stand a chance against the combined power of the Ferth family and me."

I laughed, knowing he was right. "Hopefully, we'll get him before he kills another one of our cars."

Eddie jolted to a stop, dragging me behind him as a figure stepped out from behind a tree in front of us.

My heart picked up a frantic rhythm. Eddie shoved Shakes' leash into my hand as my little dog started to bark, pinging off the sidewalk like grease off a hot griddle.

"Step into the light," Eddie demanded, his hand sliding toward his lower back. I saw the telltale bulge of his gun when he lifted his shirt and stepped back to give him room to maneuver.

A pudgy figure with wild brown hair stepped beneath the streetlight, hands lifting in surrender.

Manny!

15

"You need to help me," Manny said, his voice a shaky squeak.

I tried to move around Eddie, but he held me back with an arm at my middle. "Help you with what?" he snapped. "Is someone after you?"

Manny's gaze found mine and held, ignoring Deitz. "They tried to kill me," he said, his voice a plaintive whine. "I don't know why. I only know it has something to do with the scripts."

I frowned. "The scripts? Why..."

He shook his head. "I told you I don't know. But they tossed my place, and somebody took Patrice's script."

Pushing Eddie's arm away, I stepped closer to Manny. "How do you know they took her script?"

"It was on my desk. She'd made her notations for changes, and I was supposed to update the master and make copies. But it was gone." He frowned. "Why would they steal a production script?"

"Do you know who wrote the play?" I asked Manny. That information seemed important, though I had no idea why.

He shook his head. "Patrice kept that quiet. Whoever was bankrolling the play didn't want anybody to know."

"Isn't that a little weird?" Deitz asked.

Manny skimmed a quick glance his way and shrugged, his round face quivering with fear. "I don't ask a lot of questions. Patrice was always keeping secrets. It was her way of getting power over people." He frowned. "I told her it was going to get her into trouble one day. I had no idea it would get her killed."

"Come with us," I told Manny. "We'll keep you safe. We can put our heads together and figure out what's going on."

Headlights skimmed over the wet asphalt as a car turned onto the street two blocks away from where we stood.

Manny started backing up. "I have to go."

"No," I said, stepping toward him. "Stay..."

He bent quickly and placed something on the ground. "I kept a copy of her script for insurance purposes. See if you can figure out what they're looking for."

The car on the street took off with a squeal of

tires, and Eddie threw himself over me as shots hit the tree where Manny had been.

The car peeled away into the night, taking a turn on two wheels and disappearing into the steady traffic trailing into Hillside from Ashville.

"Did you see the license plate?" I asked as I pushed to my feet and started after Manny.

Deitz ran with me, Shakes bounding alongside like we were playing the best game.

We stepped off the sidewalk and took off running, crossing an acre of grass that spread between my street and the one behind my apartment building. We slowed to a stop when we reached another sidewalk, staring off into a sea of lawns and privacy fences. Manny was already in the wind.

Panting softly, I rubbed my head and frowned. "He's long gone." I turned to Deitz. "At least he didn't get shot," I told him.

Eddie nodded toward the sidewalk and a trail of small droplets. "I wouldn't be too sure about that."

"We need to follow the blood," I told Deitz, starting to do just that.

He grabbed my hand, stopping me. "That's a job for the cops." He pointed to the place where the droplets trailed away. "He must have realized he was creating a trail and stepped into the grass. There will still be a trail for somebody who knows how to follow it, but the police can do that better than we can."

Reluctantly, I agreed. "I'll call Argh."

"Call the Lieutenant too. He'll want to know about the contact."

I made the phone calls as we worked our way back to my street. Shakes took advantage of Eddie and me being distracted, wandering happily around in search of the perfect spot to do his business.

I hung up as we approached the tree where Manny had been. Eddie pulled a small flashlight from his pocket and flicked it over the trunk. "Bullet," he said a minute later. "I could dig it out, but it's best if we leave everything intact for Argh."

I nodded, moving closer to the base of the tree.

"Is there something there?" Deitz asked, following my line of sight.

Deitz's light skimmed over a clear plastic zippered bag leaning against the tree. Inside was a script with Patrice's name scrawled in untidy letters across the top. "I'd say this is the copy of Patrice's script Manny was talking about."

"Bless him," I said. The distant sound of sirens cut the night, and my head snapped up. "Argh's coming." I took the bag from Eddie. "Can you stay and talk to him. Tell him I was feeling dizzy or something." I started quickly toward home.

"Where are you going?" he asked, clearly unsure about separating.

"Home. I want to spend some time looking at this before Argh steals it from us."

The sirens came steadily closer. A minute later, a squad car barely slowed before whipping around the corner onto my street as if they were on their way to stop a murder.

I ducked behind a large evergreen, waiting until they'd passed before sliding into the shadows of my building and jogging toward the door.

Shakes tugged against me, no doubt wanting to join the action down the street.

"Not tonight, social butterfly," I told him. "Uncle Argh won't play nice if we go back."

After a plaintiff whine to let me know he wasn't happy, Shakes finally gave in and bounced along behind me.

To my horror, Doug and Mrs. Gerrard were standing under the awning of the front door, watching me and Shakes run toward the building.

"Dude!"

I hurried up the steps. "Inside!"

I could feel their eyes on me as I slipped past them and dove into the lobby.

"Who's chasin' ya, dolly?" Mrs. Gerrard asked. She tottered in behind me on her kitten-heeled slippers, her eyes wide with excitement. "We saw PoPo go flyin' past."

I clutched the script against my chest, panting. Fingers of pain played a concerto on my brain bumps, and nausea bloomed in my belly. I might have overdone it.

"Deitz is meeting them. Someone got shot at out there. Eddie wanted me to go where it was safe while he talked to the police." Not a complete lie. Just not the complete truth either.

Mrs. Gerrard's heavily lip-sticked mouth formed a perfect "O." Her gaze swung to Doug.

"Dude?" he said, touching my shoulder with an icy hand.

"I'm okay," I told him. "But I really need to get upstairs and lie down. My head's killing me."

"Of course, dolly," Mrs. Gerrard said. "I'll make you some nice chamomile tea. You have chamomile, right?"

I made a noncommittal noise and started up the stairs to my third-floor apartment. My legs suddenly felt like lead. Dizziness made me clutch the railing.

Without a word, Doug wrapped a surprisingly robust arm around my waist and helped me climb. "Thanks," I said, my voice breathy. "I guess the adrenaline wore off."

"Dude," he said, shaking his head.

"I know. I'm going to take a long nap when I get home."

He sighed.

The clip-clop of misfitting kitten heels behind us reminded me I wouldn't be taking that nap because I was apparently going to have company.

Doug took the key from me and opened the door. Shakes shot past into the apartment, tail high and happy. I released the leash rather than try to catch him to unlatch it. Doug helped me to the sofa and eased me down onto it. I lay back, my eyes dropping closed as I rode out another wave of throbbing pain in my head.

"Be right back," Mrs. Gerrard said cheerfully.

I didn't open my eyes. Doug pulled off my shoes and lifted my legs onto the cushions. A moment later, he covered me with the soft throw my mom had knitted me when I'd gotten my first apartment. The memory brought tears to my eyes.

"Dude," Doug said, sounding sad.

I scrubbed the tears away, opening my eyes. "I'm okay. Just really tired."

He nodded. "You want me to take that?"

I blinked. "Huh?"

"That bag you're clutching like your firstborn child."

The script! I'd totally forgotten it.

"Oh." I handed it to him. "Put it under the couch, okay? I need to read through it after my head stops spinning."

"Where are the pills the doctor gave you."

I opened my mouth to argue.

He held up a hand. "Where are they?"

Sighing, I pointed blindly toward my room. "Bedside table. But I..."

"Stop talking."

I blinked in surprise, a bark of laughter erupting from between my lips. Doug had never talked tough with me before. It was disconcerting. And, if I was honest with myself, kind of nice.

I didn't like feeling as if he was so sensitive I could break him with an errant frown.

"Here ya go, dolly," Mrs. Gerrard said as she shuffled back inside. She must have gone to her apartment to get the tea. "Chamomile will put you to rights. Just you see."

I groaned softly, watching her wide, leopard-print legging-covered backside disappear into my kitchen with a box. Her kitten heels clip-clopped across the tile floor, and she started opening cabinets.

Two pills and a glass of water appeared in front of my face.

I looked up at Doug. He spiked a heavy blond brow. "Take them."

Sighing, I did as I was commanded. A few minutes later, Mrs. Gerrard came into the room carrying a steaming mug with a teabag string hanging out the side. She set it on the table and then made herself comfortable across from me as Doug fired up my gas fireplace.

Soon, the room was toasty, the sounds of fire snapping happily across the room. I sipped my tea and, as the pills took effect, actually started to feel better.

"You have some color in your cheeks, dolly," Mrs. Gerrard said. "Can you tell us what happened now?"

"I can't, really. It's an ongoing police investigation."

She looked crestfallen for a beat, and then her painted-on brows rose up her forehead. "Is that big handsome policeman coming over? I wouldn't mind dancing the cha-cha with that one, if you know what I mean."

I arched a brow of my own. "You mean my *father*?" My emphasis on the word "father" should have shamed her into not talking dirty about the Lieutenant in front of me. But Mrs. Gerrard seemed to have lost her last filter somewhere around her seventy-ninth birthday. "That's the one, dolly. You don't mind sharing him with another woman, right?" She made a little pouty face, and I thought the chamomile might geyser up out of my stomach for an encore. I settled the mug onto the table. "I'm going to go to bed now, Mrs. Gerrard. Thanks so much for the tea."

"You sure, honey?" she asked, looking disappointed.

"I'm sure. See you tomorrow."

She didn't take my hint until Doug stood up and took her arm, helping her to stand. He glanced one last time at me as if unsure whether he should leave. I gave him a smile. "Thanks for all your help."

He nodded and the two of them left.

I dove for the script beneath the couch.

"I have no idea what a killer would want with Patrice's script," I told Deitz the next morning. We were in his truck, heading toward our next suspect's home. Having been put off by Mr. Hatfield the last time, we'd decided to sneak up on him instead of trying to get an appointment.

"Maybe it's something in the story itself?" Eddie suggested as he pulled up to the curb and stopped.

"I doubt it. The story's really kind of mundane. It's about a housewife who wrote a murder mystery based on a real-life crime and the real killer who tried to stop it from being seen."

Deitz frowned. "Is it a drama?"

I laughed. "No. A comedy. It's really pretty funny. At one point, everyone she knows is trying to kill her and claim credit for her masterpiece." I thought about the script I'd read through several times the night before. "I did get one new piece of information, though."

Deitz looked suddenly interested.

"The title was included in Patrice's copy. It's called 'Murder Ala Morgue.'"

Zeke Hatfield was mowing his lawn when Deitz and I climbed out of his truck and started toward him.

Whipping a well-used zero-turn around a row of bushes, Hatfield didn't seem to notice us until he came back our way. When he did, his head snapped up and he stopped the mower, staring at us for a couple of beats before killing the engine and pulling off his bulky, noise-dampening headset. He scowled our way. "Whatever you're selling, I'm not interested."

"Mr. Hatfield?" Deitz asked, starting forward with his hand outstretched. "I'm Eddie Deitz, private investigator." When Hatfield ignored Eddie's offered hand, he pulled it back and dug out his credentials, showing them to the hostile homeowner.

Hatfield didn't even look down at the laminated PI license. "Get off my property."

I stepped forward, eyeing the forty-something PR guy as he glowered at Deitz, seemingly oblivious to my presence. I took the opportunity to give him the once over, using my skill for reading people to ascertain how best to approach the subject of the murder with him.

Having been something of a playboy in his twenties, Hatfield had turned an abundance of charm and smoldering good looks into a brilliant start in a public relations career. He'd joined the firm as a very junior player. Within a year, he'd become a partner in the business. Another year had seen him buying out the firm's owner. He'd made the covers of *Wealth* and *Young Entrepreneur* magazines shortly afterward.

Looking now at his two-story brick home with forest green shutters and inadequately maintained landscaping, I wondered if his obvious fall from grace had anything to do with his surly attitude. Or if he just didn't want to talk about the woman who'd been pivotal in hastening his professional demise.

An attractive man with dark hair and smoldering eyes, Hatfield's former stunning good looks had softened around the edges. The artfully tousled hair just looked messy. The bedroom eyes were underscored with purple arcs. The long, lithe form had softened enough to imply excess alcohol and not enough exercise. He looked about ten years older than what I believed to be his forty-six years, and the glower on his once striking face wasn't doing anything to improve his looks.

"Mr. Hatfield," I said, offering him a smile. "I'm MayBell Ferth. How are you?"

He scanned a gaze insultingly over my form, starting at my breasts and stopping around my ankles. The curve of his lips was really more of a leer than a smile, and I stiffened my back against the oily feel of his insulting appraisal.

He finally looked at my face, and some of the insult faded from his eyes. "I know you. Patrice hated you."

I flinched. The idea that Patrice had talked about me to the man was not comforting. "She and I had our differences. But hate's a strong word."

He shrugged. "As you know, Patrice tended toward excess. She embraced the Diva moniker because she believed it made her seem confident. All it really did was make her unpalatable." His glower deepened as he fell into his own thoughts for a moment. Then he seemed to shake it off, scanning Eddie and me a look. "I know you think I killed her. I won't deny wishing I could. But I didn't. Doing that would have allowed Patrice to finish destroying my life. That wasn't going to happen. She's done enough harm already."

Apparently, he wasn't big on taking responsibility for his own actions either.

"Do you have an alibi for the time of her death?" Eddie asked.

Hatfield shrugged. "I don't know what time she was murdered, but I was with a woman from about seven pm until Midnight yesterday. She can vouch for me."

"I'll need her name and contact info," Deitz said, pulling out his cell.

Hatfield gave us the woman's name and number, and Deitz tapped the information into his phone. "Mr. Hatfield, do you know of any reason somebody might want to kill Patrice?" Eddie asked.

Hatfield burst out laughing. "You're kidding,

right? The woman was a tick on society's backside."
He nodded at me. "Even your own partner hated
her."

I opened my mouth to deny it, but Hatfield
shook his head. "Don't bother. I know about your
past, Ms. Ferth. I know the things Patrice did to you."
He cocked his head, his eyes gleaming. "Do you tell
yourself she regretted flinging you down those
stairs? Maybe you've consoled yourself with the idea
that she really didn't mean to sleep with your
boyfriend?"

All the blood left my face. I felt suddenly dizzy.
Eddie's gaze burned a hole in my back, but I ignored
him. "Unfortunately, I have no such delusions about
Patrice. But, even given all that, are you trying to tell
me you think she deserved to die?"

"Not for those things. But do you really believe
she stopped with the small-time stuff?" He shook his
head. "Patrice slit a lot of metaphorical throats over
the years. It's going to be hard to pinpoint the one
that brought on the deadly retribution."

"Thanks for your time, Mr. Hatfield," Eddie said.
He grabbed my arm and gently turned me toward
the street.

Hatfield shook his head and started to replace
his headphones. But as we reached the truck, he
called out. "Ms. Ferth?"

I turned, my gaze hard and my chin up. "Yes?"

"You're a funeral actor, right?"

I must have flinched because he smiled. "Patrice thought that was hilarious. But you can have the last laugh if you use that particular skill to catch her killer." He shrugged. "Just a thought. It's a pretty good bet Patrice's killer will attend the funeral just to make sure she doesn't come back. Like a vampire." He laughed. "In fact, as much as people hated her, he might be the only one there."

16

E ddie called a woman named Sandy Small as soon as we got into the truck. Zeke's alleged date told Deitz that she had indeed spent the vital hours of Patrice's murder with Zeke Hatfield. Still, Eddie hung up looking unconvinced.

"You didn't believe her?" I asked him.

"She seemed surprised to hear they were together, then played it off as a bad memory for dates and times."

"We'll leave Hatfield as a possibility then. He's certainly reprehensible enough to be a killer."

Eddie nodded. "Do you want to get some lunch?" I observed his profile as he wielded the big truck through heavy mid-day traffic. "Maybe just a drive-through? I hate to admit it, but my head's killing me. I think I'd like to lie down for a while."

He nodded. "Burgers or tacos?"

"Burgers." I was pretty sure crunching a taco would split my head in two. I felt him looking at me and smiled. "They're quieter."

Eddie laughed. "Burgers it is."

A heavy silence settled between us, broken only by the process of ordering our food. Eddie headed back toward my place, making quick work of the few miles. He kept glancing my way as if he had something he wanted to say.

"Just spit it out," I finally told him.

"No, it's just that..."

I gave him a look.

Deitz sighed. "She slept with your boyfriend?"

He said it with such dismay, it made me chuckle. "That was a long time ago. I'd forgotten about it." That wasn't exactly true. Patrice had never let me forget. She'd wielded the arrogant, muscle-bound oaf's betrayal like a cudgel. "Ridley was on the football team. At the time, I'd enjoyed the attention and, okay, the status of dating a football star. The truth was he'd only gone out with Patrice because my brothers confronted him when they saw him flirting with another girl. Rid didn't have a very good reputation." I shrugged. "Argh and Dash told him if he made me cry, they'd make *him* cry."

Eddie shook his head. "So he tried to make you cry? Guy wasn't very smart."

"Not very smart at all." I spoke distractedly because my gaze had caught on the big guy with the hypercritical eyes who was leaning against the car occupying Betty's old spot.

"What's Argh doing here?" Deitz asked.

He'd brought me a car. My eyes filled with tears at the sight of the cherry red Pontiac Firebird with the white vinyl roof. My all-time favorite car, once owned by my all-time favorite person. "No," I whispered, sucking in a breath. I covered my lips with my fingers, shaking my head. The world wavered behind a wall of tears. "No, no, no, no..."

Eddie parked his truck behind the Firebird, and I was out of the big vehicle before he had time to turn it off. I headed toward my brother, my face a wet glower. "You take that right back home, Mark Greggory Ferth!"

He stared down at me from his great height of six feet two inches, his usually critical gray gaze warm. "It's okay, MayB."

I winced at the childhood name. Nobody had called me that for years. "It's not okay. I can't drive her car. If I got so much as a mud spot on it...a scratch..." I shook my head, backing away from the car. "It would ruin me."

A sob escaped my mouth before I could stop it. Covering my mouth, I stared at the car like it was a snake.

Eddie moved up next to me, his hand hovering around my shoulder for a beat as if he wanted to make it better but wasn't sure how.

Argh sighed, pulling me into a hug. "She would be thrilled to know you were driving it. She wouldn't care if you scratched it. She scratched it plenty of times. You don't think a car this old looks this good by accident, do you?"

I sniffed, burrowing into my brother's comforting warmth. "I can't do it, Argh."

He kissed the top of my head. "You can. Dad agreed. It's time the car got some use again. She needs some excitement, and Heaven knows it's pretty exciting to be a car around you."

I smacked him on the chest and he grunted, rubbing the spot. "Mom would be so proud of the woman you've become, MayB. She'd want you to have Cindy Lou."

Despite basically hugging the air space around me in a failed attempt to launch his support structure, Eddie snorted. "Cindy Lou?"

With the combined firepower of the Ferth glares suddenly pointed his way, he raised his hands and backed up a step. "Love it. Great name."

I scraped away tears and sniffled, stepping away from Argh. I winced when I saw the state I'd left his shirt in. "You've got a little..." I swirled a finger in the vague area of his soggy chest.

"Tears?" Argh asked, grinning.

"Snot," I corrected, laughing at his look of horror. "Gotcha."

He reached out and rubbed his knuckles on my

head. I yelped. "Concussion, fool? Don't touch the hair. Every single follicle hurts right now."

"Follicle warning received." He offered me a set of keys. I stared at them. "Come on," Argh urged. "You know you wanna."

I snorted wetly and, at Argh's grimace, sniffed and covered my nose.

"Here," Eddie handed me a clean tissue. "For what it's worth, that car's amazing."

"You should see under her hood," I said, a smile taking over my lips. "Argh and Dad keep her pristine."

Eddie ran a hand lovingly over the car's glossy red trunk. "Does she have the firepower Betty did?"

Argh joined him at the car, launching into car talk.

I left them to it, a smile on my face as I climbed the stairs to my apartment. A residual sadness lingered at the idea that Mom's car was no longer being kept safe and clean in the extra garage behind their house. As long as Cindy Lou was there, covered with a soft tarp, we could all pretend that someday mom would return to claim her.

But she wasn't coming back. I knew that in my head, but my heart still felt a little tender from having that sliver of hope ripped away.

My phone rang as I was climbing the stairs to my floor. I glanced at the screen and smiled. It was my boss from Exit Stage Left. "Hey," I said. "Do you have a job for me?"

A phlegmy cough answered my greeting, followed by a wheeze. "I'm..." A fresh spate of coughing ensued.

I opened my apartment door and went inside. I frowned when Shakes' impatient barking didn't greet me at the door.

"Sorry," my caller gasped out. "I've got a cold." On her best days, Ruthie Colburn sounded like a two-pack-a-day smoker. She wasn't. And never had been as far as I knew. But she definitely had the voice of one. Being sick had turned her voice to wet gravel.

"No worries. What's up?" I headed down the hallway to my room, only to find an empty Pom Hilton. My pulse shot skyward. *Shakes!*

The door at the front of the apartment opened and closed. I hurried back out to the hallway and saw Eddie with the bag of food. I hit mute on Ruthie. "Shakes isn't here. Can you run next door and see if Doug has him?"

Eddie nodded.

"May?"

I unmuted the call. "Sorry. Minor crisis here." I fought panic, trying to keep my voice sounding normal.

"Well, I won't keep you. I wanted to let you know

I have a job for you. The viewing is tomorrow. Are you available?"

I wanted to say no. With everything that was going on, the last thing I wanted to do was fake my way through somebody's funeral. And there would be studying to be done before I could accurately play the role. But the bills needed to be paid. And it might just do me some good to be distracted for a while. "Yeah. Sure. Who's the client?"

"That's the weird thing."

I felt my brows lifting. "What's the weird thing?"

"He wants to stay anonymous. He's promised to pay in cash after it's done."

"Anonymous? You don't do business that way, Ruthie." Unless she stood to make a ton of money from the assignment. "Have you already accepted the job?"

"I have. And...well...the client asked for you specifically. I know this is unusual, May. But your check for this job is double what you usually get. And it's just one day's work."

"Who's the deceased?"

Behind me, the front door opened, and Eddie came in without my dog. My knees buckled beneath me.

"Let me see here..." Ruthie said in her gravelly voice.

Deitz hurried past me and disappeared into my bedroom.

Tears burned my eyes as I waited for the words I knew would come.

"Ah, yes. Here it is. Her name is Patrice Reynolds. But there's one strange request you need to be aware of."

"What exactly does the note say?" Argh asked.

"If you want your friend back, you'll give me that script. Instructions for the exchange will follow soon." I lifted my gaze to the Lieutenant, knowing his was the mind I needed to convince. "I'm going to make the exchange."

"Absolutely not!"

I sat facing the Lieutenant, clutching the baggie Eddie had dropped the kidnapper's note into after finding it on my bedroom pillow. "I have to go, Dad. They have Shakes."

"You're not going without full backup," Argh said, ignoring a glower from the Lieutenant.

I nodded. "I'm okay with that. Believe me, I'm not looking for another concussion." *Or worse*, my mind added unhelpfully. "But I'm not leaving Shakes in the hands of some maniac either."

A knock on my door made the four of us go very still.

Dad glanced my way. "Are you expecting anyone?"

I shook my head. He nodded at Argh, who moved up behind the door with his gun drawn. Then the Lieutenant motioned for me to get out of sight.

Eddie drew his gun and moved to block me from the door.

I sighed, trying to see around him.

The Lieutenant stood to the side of the door and reached to turn the knob, mouthing a countdown. On three, he threw it open, revealing a very surprised Mrs. Gerrard, who was holding a wide-eyed Shakes in her arms.

Relief made me go limp. I shoved my way around Deitz and scooped my dog out of the elderly woman's arms. "Shakes!" I said, "I was so worried."

Mrs. Gerrard barely noticed me. Her wide, lecherous gaze slid from one man to the next, and I was pretty sure she was about to drool on her shoes.

The Lieutenant reached out and gently took her arm, pulling her into the apartment.

"Oh!" she said, batting the moth-like eyelashes at him. "You're so strong. A real alpha."

Dad ignored her flirting. "Where did you find the rodent?" he asked, his voice little more than a growl.

Mrs. Gerrard wasn't even put off by his tone. Her gaze turned ever more lustful by the moment. She placed a gnarled hand on his shirt front, swaying toward him. "The poor little darling was scratching at Doug's door. I took him to my place to keep him safe until May got home."

I shared a look with Eddie, and we both started moving.

Mrs. Gerrard, her ankle-length feathery robe swaying around her bony legs, stepped aside with a dramatic gasp as we flew into the hall. I reached down and pulled the key from under Doug's Welcome mat.

"He didn't answer the door when I knocked," Eddie said as I fumbled with the lock.

The door opened, I started forward.

The first awareness that the others had joined us was when Argh grabbed my arm, stopping me from entering the apartment first. He gently pulled me away from the door, and he and Deitz went in before me, guns drawn.

Doug's apartment was silent and still. The stale aroma of smoke hung in the air and billowed from every soft surface the two men bumped in a quick search for my friend.

I stared at the pizza boxes and fast food wraps littering every surface, worry making my stomach twist.

"He's not here," Eddie said, coming out of Doug's bedroom and holstering his gun.

Mrs. Gerrard wandered in from the hallway. "Oh my, the boy isn't very tidy, is he?"

I turned to her, setting Shakes down to snuffle around the room. "Mrs. Gerrard, when was the last time you saw Doug?"

She put a finger that was tipped in blood-red polish against her lips, tapping thoughtfully. "I guess it was a couple of hours ago when he left with that man."

We all shared a look.

"What man?" the Lieutenant demanded. "Describe him to me."

"He was tall," Mrs. Gerrard said.

"How tall." the Lieutenant asked. "Try to be more specific."

Eying the men, she said. "Maybe a few inches shorter than May's honey."

We all skimmed Eddie a look. The Lieutenant glowered. Argh growled a little. Deitz's eyes sparkled with humor.

Mrs. Gerrard frowned. "He might have been playing for the other team if you know what I mean."

Dad's brows lowered in confusion, but I knew my elderly neighbor well enough to know what she was saying. Mrs. Gerrard couched everything in sexual terms. "Why do you think the man might have been gay?" I asked her.

"He had his arm looped through the pothead's arm."

"He was holding a weapon on him," I muttered.

My knees gave out on me. I sank onto the couch, a cloud of pot-scented dust assailing my nostrils and sending me into a sneezing fit.

Shakes trotted over with a hunk of pizza in his mouth and a swagger in his gait. He dropped to his belly and scooted under the couch so nobody could steal it from him. As I listened to my dog chew cold sausage pizza, panic rolled over me. "Doug's in danger, and it's all my fault."

"That's ridiculous. Why would it be your fault?" my dad asked.

I chewed the inside of my bottom lip. I'd have to fess up to absconding with evidence. The Lieutenant would be furious.

"It's *my* fault," Eddie said, his gaze finding mine. "I wanted to look at the script before we gave it to you," he said.

"What script?" Argh asked. "Are you saying you withheld evidence?" His expression and tone darkened, his hands clenched at his sides.

I opened my mouth to confess, but Deitz placed a hand on my shoulder and gave it a warning squeeze. "Manny Poe approached me when we were out walking Shakes. I chased him, but he got away. When I returned to the spot where he'd appeared, I found a script inside a baggie. I hid it and didn't tell you about it. I apologize, but I knew once you got hold of it, I'd never see it again. I needed to know what it had to do with the murder and these attacks on May."

"You idiot!" Argh shouted. "You've done nothing but endanger her. What were you thinking?"

I stood up. "Eddie isn't…"

He wrapped an arm around my shoulders. "I didn't think. I was only trying to help."

"No," I said. Shaking my head. "Eddie didn't…"

"Give it a rest, son," the Lieutenant said, talking to Argh but frowning at Deitz. "He's right. If he'd given us the script, we'd have kept it from him." However, despite my dad's words, he glared at Eddie. "What did you find in it? Anything that will help us figure out who's behind the murder and everything else?"

I opened my mouth again, knowing Eddie couldn't know anything about the script since he hadn't had time to look through it. But his words cut me off again.

"I think I know what's going on," Deitz said, studiously avoiding my gaze. "I believe that whoever wrote the play was arrogant. I think he followed the old adage and wrote what he knew. But his arrogance got the best of him, and Patrice figured it out."

"Figured what out?" Argh asked grumpily.

"The play's about a murder," Eddie said, looking from one to the other of them.

"Of course," I said, nodding. "The person who

wrote the play wrote about a murder he was intimately familiar with."

"Because he'd committed the murder himself," Dad finished for me.

"Now, all we need to do is figure out who wrote the thing," Argh said after a moment. "And potentially the only person who knows is dead. Piece of cake."

17

"**O**kay," Argh said after a moment's thought. "Then why's the killer going after Doug?"

"Leverage," Eddie responded. "He wants May out of the picture. He must believe she saw him in the theatre that night."

"I don't think that's it," I said. "If I'd seen him, I'd have given him up by now."

"You're assuming the person we're dealing with is rational," Argh said.

He was right. It was dangerous to make that assumption.

"I can't help feeling that it all comes down to the script. May is just an accessory problem to this guy," the Lieutenant said.

"Assuming that's it," Deitz said. "Why isn't he worried about the other actors? They all have scripts too, right?"

"I don't think we can assume that," I told him. "Manny let me get my copy early because I have one of the larger parts, and I'm juggling the day job at Exit Stage Left. I had to beg and cajole to get it. I'm pretty sure by the number of scripts on the table when I grabbed mine that nobody else has theirs."

"That's easy enough to check," Argh said.

"What about Patrice's electronics? Was there any communication between her and the author of the script?" Eddie asked.

Argh shook his head. "We can't find either her phone or her laptop. They've disappeared."

"I'm sure the killer took her phone," I mused. "But Patrice was very careful with her laptop. She never left it lying around."

"Her assistant would know where it was," dad said. He looked at Argh. "You put an APB out on Poe?" the Lieutenant asked.

"Of course. I know how to do my job, Dad."

The Lieutenant grunted his agreement.

"I'd like to know why Manny tried to run May down," Eddie said, frowning.

"We don't know that he did," I said. "Somebody took shots at Manny out there," I reminded him. "So, unless we have two villains, Manny's just as much a target as me."

"Are you sure the shooter was firing at Manny?" Argh asked.

That surprised me. I thought about his question and decided I was sure. "Manny was standing fifteen feet away from us, next to that big tree. The bullets hit the tree. It seems unlikely the shooter was aiming at us."

"Unlikely," Eddie agreed. "But something to consider with everything else that's been going on."

I didn't like his conclusion, but I couldn't exactly argue against it. He was right.

"Which means you have to be even more careful than you have been," Argh said. "This guy's playing hardball."

I glanced at the Lieutenant, certain he was going to try again to keep me out of the investigation. To my surprise, he didn't. He stared at the ground, hands on hips and a frown on his face. But he didn't try to keep me from contributing. Either I was wearing him down, or he knew I wouldn't back down with Doug's life on the line. "So. What do we do now?"

We all looked at Argh for direction. It was his case. My brother straightened, his expressive gray eyes sharpening as he turned his mind back to the work he knew so well and was good at. "We talk to the neighbors and see if anybody saw Doug being abducted."

I lifted my brows and my brother shook his head, clarifying, "Anybody besides the crazy cougar lady."

I snorted.

"Then we try to find cameras outside that might have caught the car, a license plate, anything that will help us find this guy."

"What about tracking Doug's phone?" I suggested.

The three men looked at me. I shrugged. "They do it all the time on TV."

Argh snickered. "Yep, we'll see if we can track his phone. But, If the guy who took him is smart, he'll get rid of Doug's phone."

I nodded in grim agreement. "What can I do?"

"You can stay in your apartment. We'll put a tracing app on your phone and see if we can get a bead on the abductor's location when he calls."

"I can't just sit on my butt while my friend's out there, scared and alone."

The Lieutenant grunted again. "I wouldn't worry about his emotional state. Judging by the smell of this apartment, your friend is probably feeling pretty laid back right now. His biggest issue is going to be fighting the munchies."

"Har," I said. "It's medicinal grade. It doesn't give him the munchies."

In answer, the Lieutenant lifted a brow and glanced at the myriad pizza boxes, junk food bags, and containers littering the floor and furniture.

A tiny burp sounded from under the couch.

I flushed.

"If we can't get a bead on him any other way, that phone call will be the only way to find your friend," Dad said.

He was right. Dangit! "Okay," I reluctantly agreed. "But if you find him, you'll let me know immediately, right?"

"Um, yeah," said Argh, not even trying to pretend he'd do as I asked.

Neanderthal.

I paced and stewed and fumed my way through the next few hours. True to his word, Argh had sent a tech to my apartment to set my cell phone up with tracing capabilities. The guy looked like he was about fourteen, complete with a pimply complexion and a voice that squeaked every other word. His name was Randall, and his pale-blue eyes blinked at us from behind oval-shaped wire-rimmed glasses as we introduced ourselves.

Randall set up the tracking equipment and the tracing app and then lost himself in video games on his phone, ignoring my restless pacing.

Eddie worked quietly in the kitchen, still trying to get a bead on Patrice's stalker.

I wished I had something that could distract me

from worrying about Doug. Shakes tried to help by bringing me his ball and dropping it at my feet. I threw it a few times without enthusiasm. He quickly grew bored by my lack of interest, and I watched his fuzzy butt bounce toward the kitchen in search of a fresh victim.

At my wits' end, I headed to my room, intending to try to lose myself in a book.

That lasted about five minutes before I was up and pacing again. Finally, feeling as if my nerves were afire and I'd start screaming if I didn't do something soon, I yanked open my bedroom door and yelped, coming face to face with Deitz.

He looked as surprised as I did, his eyes wide and his fist raised to knock. But he recovered fast, pushing into my room and closing the door behind him. "We need to go. I've got something."

I frowned. "If we leave, Randall out there will tell Argh."

Deitz slid a gaze toward the window.

I shook my head. "Three floors. Nothing to climb down on."

We thought about it for a minute. "Mrs. Gerrard!" Deitz said.

I lifted my brows in question.

"She needs us."

He waggled his brows and I grimaced. "Ew."

"Not like that, potty brain."

"Potty brain? Don't ever waggle your brows like that when talking about Mrs. Gerrard. Ew."

"Whatever. Come on." He grabbed my hand and pulled me toward the door. We rolled past Randall, pulling his bespectacled gaze from his game. "We'll be right there, Mrs. Gerrard," Deitz said into his phone. "Stay away from the water."

He hung up as I pulled the door open. "Elderly neighbor. Her apartment's flooding."

When Randall frowned in indecision, I added, "She's just a few apartments down. If my phone rings, I'll run back here to answer it."

Randall shoved his glasses up on his stumpy nose and sniffed wetly. "K."

We didn't waste any time considering if Randall was really falling for our act. Hopefully, by the time he called my brother, Deitz and I would be well on our way to wherever he was taking me.

On the road a couple of minutes later, I turned to Eddie. "Okay, tell me."

"We're going back to Manny's place."

I frowned. "Why?"

"We think the killer is the person who wrote the script, right?"

I nodded.

"That person had to have communicated with Patrice at some point, right?"

I nodded again.

"The police couldn't locate Patrice's phone or computer, correct?"

I made a rolling motion with my hand to hurry him along.

"Bear with me, May. I'm thinking this through."

"I'm with you. I'd just like to get to the point before my ninetieth birthday."

He huffed out a breath. "I've gone over the players several times, looked at their alibis, motives, and potential opportunities from every direction. I keep coming back to Manny."

"Whose truck tried to kill me, and who is currently on the lam."

His lips quivered at my overly dramatic use of the word, "lam" but he nodded. "Exactly. The only problem is that Manny's place was tossed, and he gave you the script."

"He could have tossed his own place to throw us off. And, we're assuming he intended to give me the script, but he didn't really give it to me or even tell me it was there. He could have been stashing it to come back to."

"Hard to have a conversation with bullets flying at your face," Deitz said.

"Agreed. Let's set Manny aside for now and assume he's exactly what he looks like...a victim who was in the wrong job at the wrong time."

"So we assume someone else is after him," Eddie said. "Since the author of the play is insisting on anonymity and the script seems to be central to everything, the writer appears to be the key."

"Have you checked everybody's backgrounds to see if they have writing creds?"

Eddie nodded. "Unfortunately, that doesn't help us much."

"Let's start from the top," I said. "What about Oscar Miller, our betrayed actor?"

"Miller has no obvious writing experience outside of the usual term papers and stuff from college. And, from what I saw, he carried a solid C minus in his English classes. But, he did lie to us about his whereabouts the night of the murder, so we have that."

"Technically, it was more a stretching of the truth. He did go to see Loudan that night, but he wasn't there as long as he claimed."

"Which meant he could have theoretically made it to the theatre in time to kill Patrice."

"Barely, and only with light traffic, but it's possible."

Eddie went on. "Jenna Plum is next on the list. She's a tough one. Though she has a wealthy family who keeps her in the style she's accustomed to, she spends much of her time volunteering and serving on councils to help the less fortunate in the Ashville area. She also has a Master's in Business from Yale University and can therefore be assumed to have at least some ability to write."

"But you haven't found any evidence that she writes plays?"

"None. I haven't even found a letter or a thank you card."

I smiled at that. "Moving on. What about Zeke Hatfield?"

"As you know, Zeke Hatfield is a PR guy."

I waited for Deitz to elaborate, but he didn't. So, I felt a need to clarify. "You're thinking that means he's a writer?"

"I am."

"You do realize the skillsets involved in writing PR copy and plays are vastly different?"

"I do realize that. But you asked me for writing backgrounds. That is Hatfield's background. He writes PR copy, and judging from his success and the level of clients he supports, he's very good at it."

"Point taken. And along those same lines, Lincoln Loudan might be a dog trainer, but he's also a non-fiction author and could, conceivably, also write fiction."

"But we haven't found any connection between Loudan and Patrice."

"Right. So, unless we do, we can assume Loudan's not involved."

"Which leaves us with Bradley Cooper, Patrice's ex-boyfriend, car-restorer extraordinaire, and overall unfriendly person."

Chuckling, Eddie put on his turn signal. "But seemingly not a writer."

"Okay," I said as Deitz pulled up in front of Manny's apartment and parked at the curb. "If we concentrate on the people with a connection to Patrice and some level of writing skill, we need to talk to three people again." I frowned, remembering why we were back out on the streets. "One of them likely has Doug."

"Hopefully," he agreed.

Eddie and I climbed out of the truck and headed inside. The hallway of Manny's building was empty and quiet. Everyone was likely at work.

Unlike the last time, Manny's door was not ajar, and crime scene tape projected a warning to stay out in neon yellow.

I slid Deitz a look. "I don't suppose you know how to pick locks?"

He looked offended. "Have you met me?" He pulled a set of lock picks from a back jeans pocket and started working on the lock.

Without warning, the door flew open and a long leg shot out, catching Eddie on the side of the head. Before I could react, I received a punch to the belly that took me down to my knees on the hard carpet.

I tried to lift my head to see who was running away from us down the hall, but my body struggled against an inability to draw air. I toppled sideways, gasping and clawing at the ground until the first threads of air found their way into my lungs.

Eddie started to stir around the same time, groaning as he rolled over onto his back. "What hit me?"

"A very large shoe," I gasped out, lifting a shaky hand toward the front door. "It went thataway."

But, of course, whoever had been inside Manny's place was long gone.

18

D eitz and I limped back to the truck after spending an hour looking for Patrice's computer. We were quite the pair, both of us moving like we were a hundred years old and neither of us too steady on our feet.

I glanced at Eddie as he slid behind the wheel with a soft groan. "Headache?"

He started to nod and then winced. "Yeah. You?"

"Mine never stopped hurting from the first two concussions."

He sighed. "Are you up to interviewing one of our three suspects?"

I wasn't. The idea of talking to someone who was probably going to lie and try to get around us just made my head hurt more. I opened my mouth to tell him yes, not wanting to be the weak link in our dynamic duo, but different words than I'd intended came out instead. "I have a better idea."

"Okay."

"Let's go back to the theatre. Maybe Patrice left the computer there." While we'd searched Manny's place, it had occurred to me that the computer might be in Patrice's theatre office. In fact, the more I thought about it, the more convinced I became that it was.

"The cops surely searched for it there," Eddie argued.

"Yep. Just like they searched Manny's place. Yet you and I and the killer all, apparently, thought it might still be there."

He cocked a finger at me in agreement. "To the Hillside Theatre we go."

Fifteen minutes later, I kept watch as Eddie knelt in front of the door to apply his lock picks. Skimming me an accusatory look, he said, "Did you just step to the side to avoid being punched in the breadbasket by the killer again?"

I flushed guiltily. "I'm here to back you up in all things. Way back."

"Mm, hm." He slid a worried look over the door. "If that guy comes barreling out of there and kicks me again, I'm taking his future parenthood down with me this time."

I snorted. "Yikes!"

The lock mechanism clicked. Deitz stood, his

long, muscular form easing upward like a retired MMA fighter—all aches and arthritis in a bruised and battered package. "It's open."

We both stood there staring at each other, his lips twitching. "You want me to go in first, don't you?"

"You did promise my dad you'd protect me."

He uttered a word he couldn't repeat in front of Nana Horbuckle.

Fortunately, nobody barreled out of the theatre when Deitz opened the door. I locked it behind us and followed Deitz across the darkened space to the light switch.

The room was lit only by floor-level security lights that didn't do much to illuminate the way. I bumped into the folding table where my script had been and bounced away with a cry. Rubbing my hip, I nodded toward the empty table. "This was full of playscripts when I was here before."

He nodded. "Did the cops take them?"

I shook my head. "They were all gone by the time they got here. That's probably why the killer was still here when I arrived. He even got mine. I dropped it in the curtains when he was trying to suffocate me." I shuddered at the memory.

Eddie hit a few more lights and the room lit up, the light partially swallowed by the heavy drapes and high ceilings. He looked at me. "If Patrice was going to leave the computer in the theatre, where would she have left it?"

"I want to start in her office."

"Lead the way."

Patrice's office had once been the janitor's closet, which was situated at the end of the hall. Alongside her office were two celebrity dressing rooms. Across the hall, the remainder of the cast was crammed into one larger room with a tiny half bath and lockers for personal items. Linoleum countertops ran the length of one wall in the cast room, and makeup stations were subdivided by drawer cabinets that held makeup and small beauty appliances. Bright lighting surrounded each mirror for makeup application.

The "star" rooms were mini-versions of the main dressing room, with the inclusion of comfortable chairs for off-stage relaxation and a dressing screen in one corner.

Patrice's office had been renovated from its original purpose sometime in the last decade before Patrice arrived to direct Murder Ala Morgue. Leading into the office was a vintage, four-panel door. Marred with scratches and dings from cleaning implements and heavy use, the door was so heavy it might have been petrified.

There was just enough room in the office for a tiny rolltop desk and small, armless chair. Shelves that still held a few janitorial items lined both of the longer walls. The battered linoleum floor was mostly covered by a cheap oriental rug, and a fake potted palm sat beside the door. If the decorator had hoped to give the place life by adding the plant, he or she had been sadly mistaken. The dusty plastic leaves were as depressing as the rest of the dark, dingy room. There were no windows, and the small office was lit by harsh fluorescent lighting that buzzed as we entered the room. The space was much too gloomy to actually work in. I doubted many directors spent much time there

I checked the top of the small desk, finding a power cord but no laptop. The drawers held only the usual broken pencils, dried-up pens, and paper clips, nestled among lint and scraps of torn paper.

"It looks like the computer was plugged in here," I told Deitz, holding up the cord.

He was moving things around on the shelves, looking behind them.

I took the other wall of shelves, coming up empty after a few minutes.

We stood in the center of the tiny room, glancing around. "Well, this was a bust," I said unhappily.

Eddie shifted, crossing his arms as the floor creaked beneath him, the sound muffled by the rug. "I'm not surprised. If she wanted to hide it, this wouldn't be the right spot. It's the first place anybody would look."

I nodded. "The other dressing rooms?"

He nodded and we left, turning off the obnoxious light and closing the door behind us.

We searched all three dressing rooms for the laptop, even checking inside the toilet tanks, but found nothing.

Weary and getting depressed, I dropped into a chair and stared at Deitz. "What now?"

He stood in the open area, hands shoved into pockets and eyes downcast.

Watching him, I couldn't shake the feeling that we'd missed something. But I couldn't quite grab hold of it.

"Now, we go talk to our three suspects. You game?"

I nodded, shoving wearily to my feet. We were heading back down the hallway, past the tiny office, when my brain finally put the pieces together on what was bothering me. "Hold on," I told Deitz, excitement threading my voice. I returned to the tiny office and flipped on the light, crouching in the doorway and grasping the edge of the grimy rug. Throwing it back, I sent a cloud of dust into the air. I sneezed violently. "Ugh!" Sniffling, I made a sound of delight when I spotted the unmatched square of wood on the floor.

"What's that?" Eddie asked, crouching beside me as I dug my fingernails into a crack at the edge of the square.

"*That* is what's been bothering me," I told him,

prying a square of wood from the floor. We looked down into a hidey-hole that contained a laptop. I lifted it out, grinning in triumph. "When you were standing here before, the floor creaked. But it never creaked once in the other dressing rooms. That's when I knew something was different." I'd heard rumors about the theatre staff creating little hiding spots throughout the theatre over the years. Protecting valuables was an ongoing struggle in a place where people came and went, and dozens if not hundreds of people with unknown backgrounds worked and performed. It was the main impetus for the lockers in the dressing rooms."

But the director's office didn't have a locker. There had to be a spot to put valuables.

"You're a genius," Eddie said, grinning back at me. "Let's see what's on it."

We set the computer on the little desk and immediately realized we'd need to get past the password screen. I tried every password I could think of, going all the way back to high school drama class. I even included the word "Tinkerbell." Nothing opened the computer.

Finally, we reluctantly agreed it needed to go to Argh. He had techs who could make quick work of getting into it.

"**I** can't go in there," I told Deitz as we pulled up in front of the station.

He frowned. "Why not?"

"By now, Argh knows I've flown the coop. He's just as likely to lock me up as let me leave with you again."

"Good point," Eddie said. "You wait here. Hopefully, he won't lock *me* up."

"Don't count on it," I grumped.

"If he throws me in jail, who's going to keep an eye on you?"

I shrugged. "That might work. But only if he doesn't just march out here and grab me too."

Eddie climbed out with the laptop under one arm. "You're right. Drive the truck around the block and wait for me there. I'll be back as quickly as I can." He started to leave and turned back. "And keep the doors locked."

"Yes, mother."

I did as Deitz asked, pulling the truck into a small park facing the playground. I slid across to the passenger seat to wait for Eddie. My thoughts scattered as I watched a few young mothers, probably about my age, keeping watch on their kids while they climbed the play structure and ran around in the grass. Watching them, I suddenly felt old at thirty-three. Had I made bad life choices? Didn't I want to have kids someday?

I mentally slapped myself for going there. I didn't know when the right time was to think about upending my life for a family, but I was pretty sure the right time wasn't in the middle of a murder investigation.

Tears burned behind my eyelids, running down my cheek. My emotions were a wreck, probably due to having several attempts on my life over a forty-eight-hour period. I dug in my purse for a tissue but had trouble finding one. There was a knock on the window, and I hit unlock without looking. "That was fast."

When Deitz didn't answer, I looked up, a clean tissue clutched in one hand. And just about swallowed my tongue. "Manny? What are you doing here? Are you following us?"

The doughy assistant shoved me across the truck and ran a hand through the wild tangle of his dark curls. "I'm sorry May. I really am. But it's you or me. And I don't want to die."

Okay, that didn't sound good. "What are you talking about?" I asked, my hand slowly easing toward the door handle.

Manny reached over and hit the Lock button, holding it down. He stuck a hand beneath his hoodie and came out with a gun. The hand shook slightly, which made me nervous. His finger was on the trigger. and I didn't want to startle him into accidentally squeezing it, so I lifted my hands. "I'll make a deal with you, Manny," I said. "I won't try to get out, and you can take your finger off the trigger."

He glanced at the gun. "Why would I do that?"

"It's just good gun safety," I said, my mind racing. I barely kept from wincing at how lame I sounded, but distraction was the name of the game. Deitz should be back soon. If I could keep Manny off balance for a few more minutes...

He shook the gun at me. "Start driving."

"Where to?" I didn't make a move to do as he'd demanded.

"I'll tell you once we're moving. Hurry up. I don't want to have to shoot your PI buddy."

I gulped and put the truck into reverse, my gaze sliding back toward the station a block over in search of Deitz. "Do you have my friend Doug?"

"No," Manny said, his bushy dark brows lowering. "I don't have anything to do with any of this. I'm just a victim like you."

I pulled slowly out into the street. "Then why are you kidnapping me?"

"Because the person who's been trying to kill me wants you. If I bring you, they'll leave me alone."

"You really believe that?" I asked, creeping down the street at ten miles below the speed limit.

He shook the gun at me again. "Drive the speed limit. I don't want the cops stopping us thinking you're a drunk driver."

"You think they won't kill you after you deliver me to them?"

"Obviously, I think that. Or I wouldn't be here right now."

"So, you don't know who they are?"

Silence pulsed between us.

"Manny?"

"I never saw their face."

I thought he might be lying, but I couldn't prove it. And I couldn't make him tell me.

"Turn right at the next light."

I did as he instructed. "At least you can tell me what this is all about, can't you? You owe me that since you're turning me over to a killer."

Manny thought about it for a beat and then sighed. "Yeah, I owe you that, at least."

My pulse spiked. Finally, I was going to find out who kept trying to kill me. Then, all I had to do was get away from Manny so I could do something about it.

"Turn left at the next light," Manny said.

I put on my turn signal as the light turned red. I braked to a stop.

We sat in silence for a minute.

"It's all Patrice's fault," Manny finally said.

He didn't get any further than that. Several cop cars suddenly surrounded the truck, blocking off the intersection, coming at us from an alley on the right and a parking lot on the left, and cutting off any thought of escaping from the rear.

Deitz appeared at the passenger side window, his gun trained on Manny's head. "Drop your weapon and step out of the vehicle."

He sounded just like a cop. My life choices rose up to mock me again. I'd always sworn not to have a relationship with a cop. I loved the cops in my family, but I was on cop overload. I didn't think I could have a normal, stress-free life if I loved a cop.

I shoved the thoughts away. It would be okay. I hadn't fallen for Deitz.

Not really.

Argh appeared on my side of the car, nodding toward the lock on the door. I quickly hit the unlock button and my brother whipped it open, yanking me out of the truck and pushing me down, out of firing range.

I quietly seethed that they'd interrupted my perfectly orchestrated villain confession moment.

Dangit!

I'd been so close.

19

"How'd you find us so fast?" I accuse-asked.

Argh grinned. "One of the uniforms was in the lot and saw Manny force his way into the truck. She called it in and we figured out it was you. Deitz told me where you were waiting for him." My stupid brother wagged a finger at me. "That was naughty, McBethBell. I'm of a mind to lock you up for evading law enforcement."

"Ease back, Superpatch. I haven't done anything illegal. You can't hold me.

The guys around us snickered at my nickname for Argh. Their grins disappeared as he gave each of them the patented, one-eyed glare — perfected when he was a kid and had to wear a patch over one judgmental eye because of infections.

Thus the pirate moniker.

My brother dropped onto the corner of somebody's desk and crossed his arms over his chest, settling that hypercritical gaze on me. "Talk to me. What did Manny Poe want with you? Is he our killer?"

I looked around for Deitz. "Where's Eddie?"

"He's working with the tech guys on the computer. Now talk."

Sighing, I dropped wearily into a chair. "I don't think Manny's the killer. He denies having Doug too. But someone is pulling his strings. He insisted he was taking me to someone to save his own life."

"He's trading you to a killer to save himself?"

"That's what he said."

"Nice guy," Argh said.

The air in the room suddenly went very still. Uniforms who'd been relaxed and chatting suddenly went rigid, with squared shoulders. A beat later, the Lieutenant walked into the bullpen, the intensity of his gaze locked onto me.

I bit back another sigh. "Go easy on the grim talk around dad, okay? I don't want to be locked up in a nunnery for the rest of my life."

Argh snorted. "If you tried to step into one of those, you'd be repelled on a gust of fiery air immediately. Like the demon you are."

"Har," I said, my lips twitching.

"What's so funny?" dad asked. He stopped next to my chair, towering over me as if he'd deliberately made himself taller just to intimidate me. That would have worked when I was ten. Maybe fifteen. But in my thirties, it no longer had that effect.

Mostly.

I swallowed as he glared down at me. "I didn't do anything wrong," I said, my infernal voice box giving off a squeak at the end.

"I beg to differ," he said. "Were you not told to stay in your apartment?"

I opened my mouth, but he rolled right over me.

"Were you not told to lay low until we catch this killer?"

I tried again, with the same kind of luck.

"Were those instructions unclear?"

I gave up, snapping my lips closed, and glared back at him. "I'm not going to hide in my apartment while my friend is in danger."

The Lieutenant's left eye twitched, a sure sign he was about to blow. Everybody but Argh and I suddenly found a reason to be somewhere else.

"Dad," I said, with an unfortunate whine in my voice. "I'm sorry, but Deitz and I had a lead. We had to follow it up."

He stared at me for a beat and then inclined his head. "The computer. Nice work."

I wasn't sure where to go with that, so I just said, "Thanks."

"Explain your reasoning," Argh demanded, all joking relinquished since the Lieutenant had arrived.

I reminded them of our belief that the killer was also the author of the play, and explained the subsequent exercise to determine which of our suspects might be the one. "We narrowed it down to three," I said. "We decided that our best chance of figuring out which of the three it was would be to see who's been communicating with Patrice about the script."

"I told you, we haven't found the phone," Argh said, misunderstanding me.

"I know. But with playscripts come nearly constant changes. Those changes have to be communicated, versions passed back and forth."

"And all of that activity would be on the laptop," the Lieutenant said, nodding. He looked at Argh. "Any luck breaking into it?"

"Not yet."

"There is one more avenue we can try," I told them.

Both men looked at me, waiting.

I braced myself. "Ruthie called me." When they didn't immediately show recognition of the name, I clarified. "My boss at Exit Stage Left?"

They dipped their matching square chins at the reminder.

"She says someone wanted to hire me to work Patrice's viewing." It was common knowledge in policing that perps rarely missed a chance to visit the aftermath of their crimes. There was a ninety-eight percent chance our killer would be there.

"Who?" dad asked.

I chewed the inside of my lip, knowing how he was going to take what I said next.

"May?"

I looked him in the eye. "The client wants to remain anonymous."

"No." The single word was immediate, quietly offered, and uncompromising.

"Dad..."

He shook his head, his bullish jaw jutting. "That just smells like trouble."

"Wait," Argh said, a speculative gleam transforming his gaze. "This has possibilities."

"We're not using your sister as bait," the Lieutenant said, his voice little more than a growl.

"I'm not talking about using May," Argh said, his brows lifting.

The Lieutenant's glower softened as understanding replaced it. "Ah. Now *that* I can get behind."

"What?" I said, my gaze spinning like a pinball. "What can you get behind?"

"When's the funeral?" Argh asked.

"Tomorrow sometime. Ruthie's emailing me the details."

"Good. When you get that email, forward it on to me."

"I can't do that," I said. "You're planning on sending a policewoman in, aren't you? That's not going to work. Ruthie's taking money for the job. If the client finds out you sent in an unskilled actor..."

"Who says she's unskilled?" Argh asked.

"Does she have a contract with Exit Stage Left?"

"We can work something out with your boss, Punkin'. Don't worry about that."

I sent a glare my dad's way. "Do you understand this is my livelihood? If you do something hinky, Ruthie's going to fire me."

"We won't do something hinky," Argh said dismissively. "We're trying to catch a killer, May. Don't you want that? Don't you want to find Doug?"

I faltered. "Of course I do. But the way to do that is to send me in. Not some random woman who has no idea how to cry on cue."

Argh blew air through his lips. "How hard could it be?"

I clenched my fists, feeling my entire body start to vibrate under a wave of rage.

The Lieutenant's eyes went wide. "Be quiet, Argh."

"What? She thinks it's rocket science or something. Any Schmoe can stand up there and bawl into a hankie wrapped around a fresh onion. It'll be fine."

My face burned. My cheeks were probably a fine shade of puce. The vibrating had gotten so bad, my teeth were knocking together.

"Really, son. Stop talking."

"Why? Do you think I'm afraid..."

My hand shot out so fast even I was surprised. It was a blur in the air, only the pain of my knuckles hitting Argh's face told me for sure that the fist had been mine.

Argh's head snapped back and he backpedaled, his hip hitting the desk behind him before he toppled backward, sending piles of paper and folders onto the floor.

Blood immediately welled from his nose and I didn't care. I cradled my hand and leaned over him, growling my next words. "You're a horse's backside. One of these days, you're going to understand that I have a passion for what I do. It might not be important to you, but it is to me. Don't ever dis my work again."

I turned to the Lieutenant. "The client asked for me. If someone else goes in my place, he'll know you're on to him and you'll lose this opportunity. If that happens and Doug suffers for it, I'll *never* forgive you." I swung my gaze to Argh, who was trying to stop the bleeding. "Either of you."

I didn't look back as I headed for the door. I was done trying to cooperate with my family. I was done playing nice. I was going to do my job, save my friend, and catch a killer.

Or die trying.

"May," Eddie whispered from the shadowed environs of the stairs leading down to the street. "I got in." He motioned for me to hit the stairs. "Hurry. I think I know where Doug is."

I ran in his direction, taking the steps at a reckless speed. "Why are you hiding?"

He shoved the glass door open and ushered me out in front of him. "I might have grabbed some information from the computer while the tech guy went to the bathroom. We need to get out of here."

I laughed. I couldn't help it. After the emotional blowup with my brother, it felt good to pull one over on the jerk. "Argh's going to be really ticked." I rubbed my knuckles, not even minding the pain.

Eddie wrenched the passenger side door open and helped me up. "*We* found the victim's computer, not him. He'll just have to deal."

As Deitz ran around to the driver's side, I hoped the way my brother coped wasn't to lock Deitz up and forget where he kept the key.

I didn't ask any questions until we were clear of the station. Then I turned to him. "So, what did you find?"

"There were a bunch of emails from someone with a free email service. The sender is clearly using a fake name. He called himself Edgar Allan Poe."

I felt my eyes go wide. "Poe? Could it be Manny?"

"Seems a bit on the nose. But I wouldn't put it past the guy to be trying to set Manny up."

I nodded.

"We used geolocation to find the general address. It maps to one of our suspects."

I had no idea what geolocation was, but it sounded like a good thing to know. "Who is it?"

He took a turn too fast, the truck's tires squealing. "We're hopefully about to find out."

Fifteen minutes later, I had a sinking feeling in my gut. "Manny's place?" I'd really believed him when he'd said he hadn't taken Doug.

Eddie sighed. "I thought I recognized the building address. There's probably no sense searching Manny's place again, but we should probably do it just to be thorough."

I agreed and we headed inside. As we stopped in front of Manny's door, I had a sinking feeling. "I feel like we're missing something."

Eddie made a face. "None of this makes sense."

I leaned against the wall and shoved my hands into my pockets. "What are we missing?"

I looked around the hallway, seeing the same grungy carpet and dinged-up walls as before. An overhead light flickered down the way, its light catching on something small and white on the floor beneath it.

Pushing away from the wall, I walked over and

looked down at what appeared to be part of a cigarette. Crouching down, I examined it more closely.

"What is it?" Eddie asked.

It took me a minute, but I finally wrapped my mind around what I was seeing. I lifted the cigarette to my nose, the familiar scent making my pulse spike. "It's Doug!" I said, straightening.

"Doug? What are you talking about?"

I ignored Deitz, moving quickly back the way we'd come. My gaze followed the trail of a torn doobie that Doug had left for us on the dirty carpet. The trail stopped in front of the door across from Manny's apartment.

I tried the door, finding it locked. "He's in here," I whispered to Deitz. "I'm sure of it."

Eddie gently pulled me to the side and reached over to knock on the door. Silence met his knock. He knocked three more times to make sure.

"Pick it?" I whispered.

He dropped to his knees and pulled the picks out of his pocket, setting to work. A moment later, the door was open. I started forward, but Deitz blocked me from stepping through. Holding up a finger to stall me, he slid his gun free and used the muzzle to tap the door open another couple of inches.

When nobody ran out at us, he pushed it open wide enough to ease through.

I peeked through the door and gave a soft yelp of

excitement when I saw the only thing in the otherwise empty apartment.

Still, I let Deitz clear the place before running over to the man lying on his back, tied to a chair. Doug had a blindfold over his eyes and a rag tied across his mouth. Deitz went to work on the ropes tying him there. I removed the blindfold, tugging the rag down over his chin. "Doug! Are you okay?"

His eyes had been closed, but at the sound of my voice, they'd opened, looking a little blurry. "Dude."

He sounded woozy. "Did they give you something to knock you out?"

He shook his head. "I knocked myself out. I was trying to get out of this chair."

Eddie tugged the ropes loose, and the two of us helped Doug stand. "Did you see who took you?"

"No. It was a big guy. But he wore one of those ski mask things. That schtick is so overdone, man."

I fought a grin. "Thanks for the trail. We'd have missed you otherwise."

"Dude! Did you pick up all the pieces? Maybe I can still use them."

I laughed, giving Doug a hug. "We need to get out of here."

"Yes, we do." Eddie agreed. "Before the killer comes back."

"Killer?" Doug said, clearly surprised. "But, I'm not dead, Dude."

"Not from the neck down," Eddie murmured.

20

We left Doug at his place with orders to lock up and not answer the door to anyone. Then we returned to my place, where I half expected to be arrested for absconding with evidence in the investigation.

But my apartment was empty. To my vast relief, Randall was no longer there. I headed for the kitchen and poured myself a glass of water, draining the glass in one long drink. Eddie disappeared and returned with two white pills in the palm of his hand, stretching them toward me.

I shook my head.

He moved the hand closer to my face.

We glared at each other for a few taut seconds and then I sighed, taking them. "They'll make me sleepy."

"There's nothing wrong with taking a nap. I'll

stand watch out here. I've got some research to do anyway."

"On what?" I narrowed my gaze on him. "You're not going to sneak out of here without me, are you?"

Eddie gently pushed a strand of hair off my face. "I wouldn't think of it." I closed my eyes at the warmth of his touch, my body flaring to life as I became acutely aware of his warmth, his delicious masculine smell, and the rightness of his touch.

Soft lips touched my forehead. "Go. Rest for just an hour. And then we'll start to plan out our next move."

I reluctantly agreed, my body so exhausted and my head throbbing so hard, I couldn't even make it to my room. I dropped onto my couch and fell over, my eyes already closing. Eddie covered me up and pulled off my shoes. A sense of déjà vu swept over me. I smiled, remembering how Doug had done the same for me not that long ago. At that moment, I realized something I'd do well to remember. Eddie's sarcastic point from earlier sank home. Being cared for did not suck. It didn't suck at all.

Sleep, a voice said, *Tomorrow you'll catch a killer.*

It might have been Eddie talking. But somehow, he spoke in my mother's voice.

With the words dancing through my mind, I let my body soften and the world fell away.

I awoke sometime later to the sounds and smells of cooking. I rolled upright, eyes refusing to stay open, and sat there swaying as my mind slowly began to clear. When I finally managed to wrench my eyes open, I noticed it was dark outside my windows.

Yawning widely, I reached out and stroked a hand over the soft bundle at the end of the couch. Shakes wriggled happily and went belly up, his skinny sticks poking straight into the air.

I grinned.

"Hungry?"

I looked up as Deitz came into the room, carrying a tv tray. He set it in front of me, and the spicy scent of rich tomato sauce filled my nostrils. "Mm. This smells delicious."

"My nana's recipe for spaghetti Bolognese. Eat. You need your strength."

He didn't have to ask me twice. I dug in, surprised at how hungry I was until I realized I hadn't eaten for hours.

"How's your head?"

"Much better. I feel almost human."

Eddie sat across from me in an aged, overstuffed armchair. He had his own tv tray set up and was consuming an alarming amount of pasta.

I dipped a crunchy slice of garlic toast into the

sauce and tasted it, rolling my eyes in pleasure. "You're hired."

His luscious lips curved upward. "I am? For what?"

"For cooking. For whatever." My eyes went wide as the words fell off my lips and my cheeks heated, probably matching the spaghetti sauce for their red color. "Sorry. That must be the drugs talking."

He shook his head, his forest green gaze sparking with interest. "Don't apologize. That's the best offer I've had in years."

If it was possible, my cheeks heated more.

We ate in silence for a few more minutes. When my stomach felt as if it might burst, I drank some water and sat back on the couch. I curled my legs beneath me and pulled the throw over them. "Have you heard from Argh or my dad?"

Eddie sat back too. He sipped a beer and shook his head. "Not a word. They're definitely plotting something."

"They are. They got it into their beady brains that they'd send a female police officer into the funeral instead of me."

"Ah. That sounds like something your family would do."

I shrugged. With time and distance, I understood why they thought it would work. "It makes sense if you don't look too close. The problem they have is that the client asked for me. As far as I know, they don't have any doppelgangers of me on the force. Which means, as soon as the cop shows up pretending to be me, it all goes south."

Eddie nodded. "How do you want to play it?"

"Easy. I'm going to perform the role Ruthie gives me. And we're going to figure out which of the people at the funeral want me dead. That will tell us who killed Patrice."

"Good."

"You're going to need to disguise yourself so you can mingle without drawing the killer's attention."

"Leave that up to me. I've got just the thing."

I climbed to my feet and went to get my laptop from my room. Ruthie would have sent me my assignment details, and I needed to study them.

I had a very important role to perform.

I was halfway through role prep when my doorbell rang. I glanced up at Eddie. He jerked his head toward my room. "Go. Pretend you're asleep. I'll handle this."

It was no doubt either Argh or my dad, so I didn't argue. If they thought Eddie and I were planning something, they'd take me into custody and lock me down. But, if they thought I was taking my medicine and acting the role of docile victim, they might leave me alone.

I dove under the covers and shoved the computer out of sight, listening to Argh's raised voice in my living room.

Eddie's response, by contrast, was pitched low and much calmer.

A minute later, I heard footsteps in the hallway. My eyes snapped closed as the door opened.

I lay there, feigning sleep, my skin crawling from the sensation of being watched. Fortunately, it didn't last long. The light from the hallway eased away as Argh pulled the door shut again. "She took her meds?"

"She did. She'll sleep all night. I'll stay here to make sure nobody bothers her. What exactly do you have in mind about the viewing tomorrow?"

"That's none of your concern. You're lucky I don't arrest you for taking evidence and running with it."

I could almost see Eddie shrugging. "We saved Doug. Nobody was hurt. We're on the same side, Ferth. I'm just trying to find the person who wants to hurt May...same as you."

Argh's answering silence told me he couldn't disagree with Eddie's motives. "Keep her here until early afternoon tomorrow, understand?"

Eddie must have nodded because I didn't hear him respond. He'd better have had his fingers crossed behind his back because I had no intention of hiding in my apartment while a killer ran free. Not if I could stop him.

I climbed out of bed when I heard the front door close. Emerging from my room a beat later, I looked at Eddie. "On a scale of one to twenty, how mad is he?"

Deitz shook his head. "You don't want to know."

I went back to reading my notes from Ruthie. The suggestion of my acting a part I'd lived in real life was unpalatable. I chafed at the idea. Patrice would have loved my discomfort, of course, which only added to my reluctance to do it.

I'd played difficult parts before. But not in a way that dug into my own lifelong insecurities. Fortunately, the instructions would work to my advantage. Though, I couldn't help wondering what the killer hoped to gain from the show.

"I discovered something interesting in my research tonight," Deitz told me, interrupting my concentration.

I looked up, trying to keep impatience from my expression. "What?"

"I don't know if it pertains to the current situation at all, but Jenna Plum and Patrice had an affair that ended badly."

My eyes went wide. "Jenna Plum? Really?"

He nodded. "Jenna was in her early twenties. Her family paid people off to keep it quiet for obvious reasons. Not only was Patrice not the kind of girl they'd hoped their daughter would bring home to dinner, but she was unpredictable and volatile, a toxic personality. They had too much to lose if

Patrice went on an emotional bender and dragged Jenna into it."

"I can certainly understand that." Wherever Patrice went, trouble soon followed. "They paid Patrice off?"

Eddie nodded. "Jenna must have pitched a fit because they shipped her off to live with an Aunt in France right around that time. She stayed there for ten years."

Yikes! "Sounds like she was really mad."

Deitz grunted in agreement.

"I'd like to talk to Jenna this morning. I'm assuming she'll be at the viewing."

He nodded. "If that's the case, we'd better get moving."

I stood on the sidewalk in front of Holmes Brothers Funeral Home and closed my eyes, my stomach queasy with worry over my upcoming portrayal. Of all the roles the client would request that I play, spurned friend and longtime rival seemed the most diabolical because of its proximity to real life.

Pulling air into my lungs to soothe my nerves, I released it slowly and opened my eyes. "You can do this, May," I told myself, clutching the wriggling little furball in my arms. I looked down at Shakes. "Ready, buddy?"

Decked out in his faux diamond finery and a fluffy white sweater we saved for only the best occasions, my little sidekick gave a happy yip, his silky waterfall of a tail wagging enthusiastically.

Straightening my shoulders and lifting my chin, I donned my carefully crafted persona and climbed the stairs to the double doors.

"I'll get it for you, dear," an older gentlemen with a bent back and an uncertain gait called out behind me.

The man struggled up the steps, but I forced concern from my features and waited, Shakes wriggling with excitement in my arms. "Yip!"

"Such a handsome young man," the elderly gentleman said, giving Shakes a scratch between his tiny, triangular ears. The man's gaze caught mine, twinkling. "A fitting companion for such a lovely young woman."

I inclined my chin, sliding my gaze toward the door in a silent request.

The man struggled to pull the heavy door wide. Shakes and I stepped through, striding confidently into the room where Patrice Reynold's body was laid out for viewing. As we entered the room, all eyes slid our way, a few widening at the sight of my pampered little companion. Ignoring them all, I strode toward the casket at the back of the long, narrow room.

Patrice's treasured curls were spread artfully across soft pink satin. She lay in perfect repose in a casket of pure white, with golden handles and end caps. She wore a gown from a fairytale, looking every bit like an enchanted princess.

Even in death she played a part.

I stared down at her, my stomach twisting with nerves for what I was about to do.

"She almost looks human, doesn't she?" a familiar voice said. I turned to find Bradley Cooper frowning down at his deceased ex. "I have a new respect for the corpse-gilding abilities of undertakers."

I bit back the urge to upbraid him for his course statement. Unfortunately, my role required me to join him in the attack. "The princess routine is rather galling," I said, forming my lips into a sneer. "I'm surprised to see you here."

His smile was mean. "I guess a part of me just wanted to make sure the witch was dead."

I turned a shocked look his way, finding him staring at Patrice with suspiciously shiny eyes. "I'm sure her killer would understand that sentiment," I said, testing the waters.

If my insinuation sank in, he didn't let it show. A moment later, I drifted away from Patrice, my gaze skimming over the assembled group. I spotted the elderly man who'd helped us with the door and inclined my head at him. He was standing with a distraught blonde woman who looked a lot like Patrice. Next to her was a clearly bored younger man who didn't look at all like he could be Patrice's brother, making me think that Mrs. Reynolds was a very naughty woman.

I spotted Zeke Hatfield standing with his hands in his pockets, leaning against the back wall. He acknowledged me with a tip of his chin and then slid his gaze away, people-watching but not speaking to anyone.

My gaze skimmed over another familiar face. A decidedly hostile one. I gave Argh a smile and a little finger wave. His hypercritical gray gaze turned as brittle as ice. Beside him, I recognized Dani Kraft, Argh's girlfriend. Dani wasn't police, but she was the next best thing. A kick-butt security professional. She wore a red-gold wig over her white-blonde bob and was dressed more like me than I currently was. Keeping to character, I'd donned a pink suit with a short pencil skirt instead of my usual funeral fare of black slacks and a black silk blouse with pearls.

I winked at Dani and she gave me a crooked smile, no doubt appreciating me getting one over on my brother much more than he did.

With her role impersonating me off the table, I saw Dani relax enough to clasp Argh's hand and whisper something in his ear that made his teeth stop grinding together.

I was glad they were there. It was good to have

backup.

I caught my brother's eye and jerked my head toward Cooper. His eyes flashed with irritation, but he and Dani strolled in the hostile ex-boyfriend's direction. Of my original three suspects, only Zeke Hatfield was there. A disappointing but not too surprising occurrence. From my extended suspect list, only Cooper had arrived.

Oscar Miller's attempt to present himself as a good guy thespian with altruistic interests took a hit when Patrice had deliberately sabotaged him. He'd be stupid to show up at her funeral when he was trying to extricate himself from her poisonous aura.

And that left Jenna Plum. What was her story? Did she just not care enough about Patrice to show up for her viewing? Or was she still holding on to old heartache? Either was possible, but Jenna Plum didn't strike me as a woman who let others dictate her happiness.

Sunlight flared across the entryway carpet. I glanced up to find the woman herself coming through the front doors. Apparently, she cared after all. Jenna kept her head down, and she looked pale. She moved into the room, striding quickly toward the casket at the back of the room. I hurried in that direction, intending to have a word with her before she left.

"Such an adorable pup," said a woman with a quivery voice. Before I could dodge away, a tiny woman with an elaborate bouff of soft white hair stepped in front of me, her gnarled hand lifting toward Shakes. She had the good sense to stop before petting him, lifting a watery brown gaze to my face. "Is he friendly?"

Before I could nod, Shakes licked the woman's fingers, and she was lost. With a happy gurgle, she cradled his tiny face in one hand and allowed him to kiss her nose as she scratched under his chin.

A moment later, two of her friends had joined the fray and I realized I'd totally lost control.

Head down and not looking at anyone, Jenna slipped past our little group, heading toward the Ladies' room across the hall.

I caught Argh's gaze across the room, my eyes pleading for rescue. He laughed at me.

Jerk.

I finally managed to extricate myself five long minutes later, just in time to be confronted with someone from my past. Horror twisting sharp fingers in my belly, I looked up into the golden-brown orbs of Ridley Yernst, Hillside High's star quarterback and my ex-boyfriend.

The ex that Patrice had slept with behind my back and had then spent years beating me about the head and ego with to ensure I never forgot how inadequate I was.

My mind went back to the "strange request" the client had required for the professional mourner job. I'd taken the job despite the unpalatable request. I'd had to. But I was determined not to play it the way the client wanted. I just hoped Ruthie wouldn't suffer for it. I didn't want to lose my job.

Across the room, I saw Argh stiffen and start forward. Catching his eye, I shook my head. The last thing I needed was for him to come to my rescue and mess up my plan.

"MayBell?" a deep voice drawled. "Is that you? You look amazing."

I stepped close and lowered my voice, letting my body language portray the hostility the client had requested. "Ridley, why are you here?"

Despite my trying to keep a low profile, all conversation stopped, and all eyes turned our way. Out of the corner of my eye, I saw Argh start forward again, but Dani grabbed his hand and stopped him.

Rid's mouth opened in apparent shock. It was clear he'd expected me to play along as directed. He glanced around the room, his fair complexion pinkening. "Um, can we not do this here?" He spoke in a voice that carried across the room, though his words implied he didn't want others to hear. If a small part of me had doubted he was a willing participant in the scene, I no longer held out hope of that.

I fed a little more fire into my eyes and voice. "You shouldn't have come. But, since you're here, pay your respects and leave."

Ridley crossed his muscular arms over a truly stupendous chest. I noticed he hadn't grown out of his tendency to showboat all his assets with tight shirts and tighter jeans. "That stuff with Patrice was a long time ago. It meant nothing to me," he insisted. "You need to get over it."

Someone gasped at his less-than-gallant words.

I stared hard at him, knowing if I spoke I'd say all the things I didn't want to say. Tears of anger slipped down my cheeks, prompting a couple of the little old ladies to verbally object. One of them stepped toward Ridley, shaking a tiny fist. "You need to leave, young man." Her friends nodded enthusiastically.

"Yip!" Shakes added, followed by a growl.

Rid looked around the room, found himself outnumbered, and ducked his head. "I'm sorry, May." He lifted his gaze, his eyes filling with warmth. "I really am."

I sniffled, scrubbing at my face with a hanky I'd been handed by the helpful elderly guy who'd opened the door for me. He'd joined the fray and decided to weigh in. "I have no idea what you did, and I don't need to," the old guy told Rid in his shaky voice. "But, you should go on out of here, son. Your presence is only causing problems."

Ridley threw one last look at me and spun on his heel, striding out into the sunshine.

With a heart-rending sob, I handed Shakes to the elderly man and ran out of the room. I headed directly across the hall to the Ladies' room. Plunging through the door, I expected to find my target on the other side.

But the woman who walked out of the nearest stall and turned to me in shock as I burst through the door was not who I'd expected.

Molly Baucht stared at me for a beat and then smiled. "Oh, Ms. Ferth. You startled me." The smile slid away as she took note of my disheveled and slightly soggy state. "Are you okay?" She washed her hands as I moved to the sink and splashed cold water over my face.

"I'm fine, Molly. Thanks. I was actually hoping to run into Jenna. I saw her come in but got distracted."

Molly nodded, drying her hands on a paper towel. "She was here a couple of minutes ago." Molly frowned. "I'm surprised you didn't run into her. She told me she was going to give Patrice a quick view and then leave."

Molly's plump mouth pursed with displeasure. "That seemed a little cold to me, but..." She shrugged, flinging the wadded-up paper into the trash. "Jenna's not real sentimental."

"She seems very driven."

Molly barked out a laugh. "That's certainly one word." She frowned as if regretting her words. "I'm sorry. Ignore me. I really do like Jenna. It's just, sometimes she can be a bit ruthless."

Was Jenna's assistant trying to tell me her boss

was capable of murder? "How ruthless, exactly?"

Molly went very still, her eyes widening for just a beat, and then she gave me a sad smile. "You're wondering if she killed that Patrice woman?"

"It crossed my mind, yes."

Staring past me as if lost in a memory, Molly hugged herself as if she were cold. She rubbed her arms and finally looked my way. "She might as well have."

My pulse spiked. "What do you know about the murder, Molly? Do you know something that will help me find the killer?"

Molly expelled air, her eyes glossy with unshed tears. She sniffed and finally nodded, reaching for a dark purple clutch purse. Wheezing softly, she pulled an inhaler out of her purse and used it. "I didn't want to get involved."

"I know," I said, taking a step closer and adapting a soothing tone. "But I'd be really grateful for your help."

Tears slipped down Molly's smooth cheeks. She sniffed again. "You would?"

I nodded, and she gave me a tremulous smile. "Okay." Her hand dipped into her purse again and came out with a gun. Like magic, the tears disappeared. "Oops. This probably isn't the kind of help you wanted, huh?" She lunged for me, grabbed my arm, and twisted it behind me, jamming the muzzle of the gun into my side.

I yelped in pain as she shoved me toward a door I hadn't noticed before. On the wall across from the sinks, the panel was painted the same color as the walls, making it blend in.

Molly jerked the gun toward a small latch midway down the panel. "Open that up, and hurry. The way the people out there are sucking down coffee, somebody's going to have to come in here soon."

"Molly, I don't..."

Wheezing softly, she jammed the gun under my chin, hard enough to leave a bruise. "No talking. Move."

I opened the door and pulled it wide. Molly shoved me into what looked like a supply closet. Fear sent rivulets of cold sweat sliding down my spine. "Look, Molly, don't do anything drastic."

She shoved me again, and I realized there was another door at the back of the long closet. "Open it."

The second door opened onto a dark stairwell leading down into a cold but well-lit room. In the bright, fluorescent lighting below, I could see shiny stainless steel tables and carts filled with tools.

Molly made a move to push me again, so I started down the steps, moving more quickly than she expected. If I could just get onto flat ground before she did...

From behind us, the distant sound of scratching

and whining told me Shakes was on my trail. I stumbled as I started to turn and lost my footing, tumbling down the last few stairs. Pain lanced through my back and elbows as I hit the hard, cold tile at the bottom.

"Yip!"

Shakes!

Molly stopped on the bottom step and swung her arm toward the door at the top. "You'd better hope he didn't come with a friend who'll open that door. I'll shoot the little furball before he can even get to you."

I eyed the distance between her and the door, wondering if she could make the shot. I wouldn't risk it. "I'll cooperate. You don't need to hurt him." Hopefully, Deitz would figure out why Shakes was so frantic to get through that door. I just needed to stall. More importantly, I needed to draw Molly and her gun away from the stairs.

Backing away from her, I held my hands in front of me and played the docile victim. "Why are you doing this?"

Molly smiled, strolling after me as if she had all the time in the world. I couldn't help wondering what she knew that I didn't. "I used to work in this funeral home when I was in high school. I told you that before, didn't I?

She had. I mentally kicked myself for not paying closer attention.

"They actually have a great intern program for Stem students." She reached out and punched a code into a security panel. A stainless steel barrier slid across the stairwell opening. A grinding sound drew my gaze to a second partition sliding over what I assumed was the main access door to the morgue.

"For example, I learned that the previous mortician, who was a woman, had a violent ex-husband who threatened her life on a regular basis. Guy was a real psycho. He particularly had daydreams about killing her in her own morgue. Sick son of a gun, amiright?" She laughed. "So this mortician spent a lot of money putting safeguards and back doors into her workroom." Molly's smile was mean. "Unfortunately for you, the security can't be overridden from above."

My gaze slid to the panel on the wall, and my thoughts started spinning over possible passwords.

Molly saw me looking. "Aw, that's adorable. You think you're going to get the chance to try a password or two?" She shook her head. "Nah. You'll be dead long before that happens. Just like Jenna." She jerked the gun toward a table on the other side of the room, where a large body covered in a sheet rested. I knew it was a body because of the hand that spilled from under the sheet, hanging over the edge.

Nausea bloomed in my belly. I bent over and retched, emptying my stomach of everything I'd had to eat or drink all day.

"Oh darn," Molly said.

I dragged a hand over my mouth and lifted my head to look at her. She was staring at a series of monitors over our heads. One monitor on each end was blank. The three in the middle displayed the entranceway, the sidewalk, and the parking lot outside the building. All of them showed the viewers from upstairs leaving. I spotted Argh and Eddie talking on the sidewalk. A moment later, Argh climbed into his car and left.

Eddie glanced at his watch and waited.

Panic clawed my chest. Why did my brother leave? Why was Eddie just standing there? Didn't they realize I was missing?

"They'll never find you down here." Her too-white teeth gleamed in my direction. "Even if they figure it out, they won't be in time."

"You'll be trapped here with me," I reminded her.

"Not if I look like a victim too."

I realized she intended to hurt herself somehow and then claim the killer left her to die with us. "My family won't believe you. They'll dig until they find the truth."

Molly shrugged. "We'll see."

Tears streamed down my face as a large SUV drove up to the curb and slammed to a stop. The Lieutenant climbed out and stalked over to Eddie, his big form rigid with anger. Two more cop cars screamed up, their lights and sirens going, and stopped near the Lieutenant's SUV.

Deitz had a wriggling Shakes clutched in his arms, his manner stiff and outwardly calm. A shouting match followed, where it seemed everyone disagreed with the next steps. Then, some kind of agreement appeared to happen and, within minutes, everyone had jumped into cars and hared away, chasing some nonexistent boogie man.

An icy dread made it hard for me to move. My stomach twisted with fear, and tears fell unheeded. I sat back on my heels, unwilling to just give up. There had to be a way out of the mess I found myself in. I needed to get the gun from Molly and subdue her. Then I'd have to find a way to communicate with Deitz or Argh.

My phone!

My hand slipped into the pocket of my slacks and Molly laughed. "You don't really think that will work down here, do you?"

Hope crashed and burned. She was right. The place was like a bunker.

"Okay, you got me. I'm helpless and you're going to kill me," I said, my voice a defeated murmur. "At least tell me why? Why did you kill Patrice? Why Jenna? And why me?"

Perched on the edge of an empty autopsy table, Molly seemed perfectly relaxed. We could have been just two women having a nice conversation, except for the madness in her eyes. "I learned a lot of things in this place, you know. I also heard a lot of stories. Working with dead bodies is fascinating. You see, each dead body comes with a story. Some of the stories would make great movies."

An inkling of understanding sprouted in my brain.

"Turns out, one story did make a great play. There was just one problem." She turned to glare at the sheet-covered body across the room. "Jenna was snooping around my computer and found the play. She must have liked what she read because the next thing I knew, she was getting emails from someone named Patrice about a production Jenna was sponsoring. For charity. Isn't that nice? They wanted to help people." Molly's face transformed into a mask of rage.

"That witch stole my play and was going to produce it under her own name. She was going to take everything from me. My dreams of getting published. Everything. Then, to make things worse, she told me my position was ending. She was firing me!"

I winced. Of course, Jenna was going to fire the one person who could tell the world she'd stolen the play she was going to represent as hers. "I'm sorry. That's really stinky," I said.

Molly surged off the table and started to pace, the gun in her hand flying around as she gesticulated angrily. "I've given that horrible woman ten years of my blood, sweat, and tears." She laughed angrily. "I even gave her a future as a playwright."

"It was you Patrice was meeting that night, wasn't it? You're the MB in her calendar."

Molly just stared at me.

Patrice had lied to Deitz about who she was meeting, then something must have spooked her, and she called him. "What did you do to scare her? She called the PI she'd been working with and told him she was scared. Someone was stalking her. It was you, wasn't it?"

"Of course it was me. Patrice made that appointment to meet at the theatre, knowing you'd be showing up around seven. She wanted you to see me there, hoping I'd kill you and the PI would catch me in the act. It didn't quite work out for her. I got there early and heard her calling the PI."

"That's why you killed Patrice?" I asked, scanning the room for a path that would take me away from Molly.

"I went to her after I realized she had my play. I confronted her. She and Jenna had cut a deal where she'd produce the play, and Jenna would bankroll it. They'd share the acclaim. Jenna didn't want her name connected with the production until after it was a smash hit." Molly snorted. "Jenna always got what she wanted. And she wanted to make sure it was a success before she took credit. I told Patrice I knew what Jenna had done and threatened to go to the news with it. Jenna's family would have killed her if this had gotten out. I tried to get Patrice to change the playwright's name to mine." Her face turned to a mask of rage. "She tried to bribe me." Molly's lips curved in a mean smile. "So, I named an exorbitant price. I would have taken the money and gone away. But Patrice didn't deliver the cash."

Another puzzle piece fell into place. At least I knew why Patrice had gone to Bradley Cooper for money and why she'd tried to set Molly up when she couldn't get the cash. "Why didn't she go to Jenna for the money?"

Molly shrugged. "I have a feeling she was afraid Jenna would pull the script. Patrice would lose her chance to direct."

I glanced at the sheet-covered body and thought that Jenna certainly hadn't gotten *everything* she'd wanted. I was pretty sure she'd want to be alive.

"And me?"

"You saw me that night at the theatre. Besides, you were helping that bushy-haired guy protect Jenna. All I wanted was the scripts. I didn't want the play to be traced back to me. But he gave you one. For all I knew, you two were going to produce it under your own names since I'd done all the dirty work getting rid of Jenna and that Patrice chick." She tapped the gun on her leg, looking smug. "I did try to warn you that day outside your place. You didn't listen. It's your fault you're going to die."

Her reasoning was totally illogical, but that didn't matter. In her twisted mind, it had been enough for her to target both me and Manny.

Molly succumbed to muttering, still pacing, still waving the gun around. She seemed to have forgotten about me for the moment.

A murky sort of plan had been forming in my mind as she ranted. I used her distracted state to duck beneath the next table and crawl from it to a metal rolling cart. I was heading toward the main door into the morgue, praying some cell service might leak through if I got close enough to an outside wall.

It was a small hope, but it was better than nothing.

I tucked myself behind the cart and pulled out my phone. One bar. I quickly tapped *911 morgue* into the phone.

"MayBell?" Molly called in a singsong voice. "Where are you?" She laughed, and the sound turned me icy with fear. The woman sounded unhinged.

I started to scoot toward a wall of cold drawers, wondering if I could get inside one of them before she could reach me. Could I brace the drawer from the inside somehow to keep her out? Maybe if I could hold her off long enough, she'd leave.

Something moved in my peripheral vision. I jerked my head that way and felt my eyes go wide. A black, tubular object with a tiny mirror on the end slid back out of view.

Someone was out there!

"Here, MayBell, MayBell..."

Molly was heading right for the door. I had to divert her attention. I shoved the cart and jumped to my feet, staying as low as I could as I ran toward poor Jenna on her table. Bullets tore past me, pinging off stainless steel and ripping into walls and equipment. I threw myself to the floor and slid like I was stealing home in a baseball game. My feet slipped beneath Jenna's table just as Molly started firing again.

Across the room, a door slammed open and Argh's voice rang out. "Police! Drop your weapon."

Molly spun around, her expression shocked. "How did you...?"

"Drop your weapon," another voice said. Relief sank through me as I realized the cavalry had truly come to my rescue.

"Drop the gun!" Argh barked out.

But Molly had other ideas.

She turned toward me and started to lift her gun, aiming it at me.

21

"No, Molly!" I screamed, knowing how it was going to end. Argh cleared the door, his gun raised. Behind him, three more cops filled the doorway, guns targeted on Molly.

An elderly man ran through the door behind them and grabbed the rolling cart, shoving it hard, right at Molly. She yelped as it crashed into her and went down underneath it as a hail of bullets pierced the spot where she'd been standing.

"I'm coming out!" I yelled and leaped to my feet, running toward Molly.

Someone else got there ahead of me. The elderly man kicked the gun away from Molly's outstretched hand and then stepped on that hand as Argh ran to me. "Are you okay?" my brother asked, looking twitchy.

I nodded, watching a uniformed officer cuff Molly and drag her to her feet.

"I swear, MayBell," Argh started, his face the picture of worried rage.

"Thank you." I grabbed him and gave him a suffocating hug, holding on for a really long time. He hugged me back just as hard.

"Yip! Yip! Yip!"

Shakes hit my calves and bounced up and down, eyes bright and excited. I plucked him off the ground and buried my face in his soft sweet fur, sighing. "Thanks for telling them where I was, buddy."

"We had to drag him away from that door," Deitz said.

I lifted my face out of Shakes' fur and smiled at my PI. Reaching out, I tugged on a strip of rubbery skin that had come loose from his face. "You're molting."

Deitz grimaced, tugging the elderly man mask off his handsome face. He'd already lost the gray hair and the sweater that made his middle look thicker.

I tugged on a strand of his midnight hair. "You make a pretty dashing old guy."

He laughed, waggling his brows at me. In his wobbly old guy voice, he said, "You want to go on a date?"

I looped my arm through his. "Good idea, let's go play Bingo."

"Ah, Tish, you're such a temptress."

Laughing at his Tish and Gomez Addams reference, I jolted to a stop just outside the door, finding myself face to face with the Lieutenant.

We stared at each other for a long moment, his granite face as devoid of emotion as his brown gaze was full of it.

I finally gave him a one-armed hug, Shakes wriggling between us. "Thanks for coming to my rescue, Dad."

He took a deep breath and let it ease out between us. "I was really scared there for a minute, Punkin."

I nodded, tears welling again. "It's okay. I'm fine."

He shook his head. "Don't ever do that again. You hear?"

"Promise."

After another minute, he pulled back and plucked Shakes from my arms. "Good. Because you seriously put the rodent in danger with your shenanigans."

I barked out a surprised laugh and followed the big scary Lieutenant out of the building, carrying his favorite yappy dog.

A fresh-faced uni trotted up and grinned at my dad. "Who's your little friend, Sir?"

The Lieutenant fixed the unfortunate fiend with a look that might have melted his face right off if we were living a Hollywood movie. Luckily for the uniformed cop, it only scarred him with bright red cheeks. He scurried away as fast as his feet could carry him.

———

"Okay, first of all, tell me how you found me," I said later after Jenna's body had been collected and Molly Baught had been processed and jailed.

We were sitting at my house because I'd had to bring Shakes home, and I'd wanted to check on Doug.

Argh looked calmer than he'd been when he'd busted into the morgue and saved me from a person who I'd come to accept as a true psychopath. He also finally seemed able to talk to me without a growl in his voice. "When you left the viewing room, Dani went looking for you. She found Shakes scratching frantically at the bathroom door, but by the time she got to the door leading downstairs, it had been sealed."

I held up a finger. "I watched you all leave."

He nodded. "The Mortician who owns Holmes Brothers now made some changes to the previous owner's strange security system. He added an exterior pad so the doors could be opened from his office and the cameras could be managed too."

I thought of the two blank screens. "You turned two of the screens off."

He nodded. "Those showed the office and the main entrance to the morgue. We were counting on Molly being either too distracted by what she was doing to notice or ignorant of which cameras were which. It was a risk, but we decided it was one worth taking."

"Did you have trouble opening the sealed door?" I asked. "It took you guys forever."

Argh turned gray. "No. Unfortunately, we needed enough of a distraction that we could get it open before Molly heard or saw us. I was afraid she'd use you to escape, or worse, kill you if she saw she was about to get caught."

"We had cops getting into position at the other door," Eddie broke in. "They were going to distract her. But you made that unnecessary when you inspired her to shoot up the room." He shook his head. "That was a pretty good distraction, but you cut it a little close," he scolded.

I shrugged. "I saw the mirror thing under the door and figured I'd better pull her attention away from you."

Eddie nodded. "Nice work, Detective Ferth."

Argh's gaze shot up. "Don't you dare encourage her!" My brother reached out and clasped my wrist. "May, if you ever pull something like you did today again, I swear the Lieutenant is going to lock you in your room and slide food trays under the door until you're too old and decrepit to get into trouble."

I shrugged. "That could take a while. Look at how that old guy saved Molly's life by flinging a cart at her today." I winked at Deitz.

Eddie laughed.

My smile died when I looked at Argh. "I'm sorry I scared you guys."

"You were told to stay home."

I nodded. "And I decided that didn't make sense."

We glared at each other for a minute. Argh finally threw up his hands. "Stubborn!"

"It runs in the family," I reminded him.

He just shook his head and started for the door. He stopped with his hand on the knob, turning back. "FYI. I read the play. Molly could have been the housewife in the story. Jenna and Patrice could have definitely been two of the characters. Everything that's happened here could have been in that play, with a few unexpected twists."

"Yeah," I said. "I know. It's just too bad we didn't know the ending before we got to it."

Argh left, leaving Eddie and me sitting in contemplative silence on my couch. Shakes snored on the cushion between us, his skinny little picks straight up in the air. I reached over and rubbed his soft belly, grinning at him.

"So that was Molly who attacked you in the theatre," Deitz finally said.

I nodded.

"And she's the one who damaged Betty too."

I grimaced. "Poor Betty. She should go to prison for that if nothing else."

"Argh looked into the lease on that apartment across from Manny's. Molly's name was on the agreement. She's apparently been planning this for a while."

"Was she living there?"

"I don't think so. It was a handy spot to watch Manny's place so she could stalk and terrify him. And for hiding Doug, obviously."

"Poor Doug," I said.

Eddie nodded. "And poor Eddie too."

I flashed him a look. "Why poor Eddie?"

He looked appalled. "Really? Do you know how much heat I'm going to take from your family for the rest of my life? They're all blaming me for your antics. And for your plan to draw out a killer."

I winced. "It didn't quite go as planned."

Eddie laughed. "Understatement. What was the deal with that guy at the viewing?"

I had to think about who he meant for a minute. Then it hit me. "You mean Ridley? Ruthie told me the client wouldn't consider the job complete unless I staged that fight. The goal was to show everybody what a jerk Patrice really was. I soft-sold it as best I could. Patrice was a jerk, but nobody should be ridiculed at their own viewing."

Eddie nodded. "Agreed." He dropped an arm

over the couch behind me. "Any idea who the client was?"

"I'd lay money on it being Zeke Hatfield. I got the feeling he was only there to see Patrice's reputation take a hit. I hope Ridley didn't mind becoming a clown again because of Patrice. He ended up being used as a pawn just as he had in high school."

"Poor Ridley," Eddie said.

"Poor Ridley was paid handsomely for that little acting job. Don't feel too sorry for him. Though, he did text me a while ago to ask me out." I grimaced. "So there is that."

Eddie's arm dropped around my shoulders. "Are you going out with him?"

I shrugged, avoiding his gaze. "He does really fill out a tee-shirt nicely."

Deitz glared over at me for so long, I thought I was going to ruin the joke by laughing. Finally, I turned to him and acted surprised. "Oh, does that make you mad?"

His glower deepened.

I leaned in, cupping his chin in one hand. "Poor Eddie."

He grabbed me around the middle and dug his fingers into my soft underbelly, making me scream as he tickled me in all my most sensitive spots. "Stop, stop, you're killin' me!" I yelled.

Shakes jumped up with an indignant yip and scurried out of the room.

I yelped as Deitz gave me one last tickle and fell backward on the couch, panting.

Eddie leaned over me. "Killin' you, huh?"

I nodded, a grin curving my lips.

He lowered his mouth to within a breath of mine. "Poor May," he said in a husky purr. And then he kissed me. And I forgot all about murders and plays and old boyfriends in too-tight tee-shirts.

DON'T MISS OUT

Stay up on all Sam's news by joining her newsletter, and get a copy of a fun mystery just for signing up!

SIGN UP HERE: https://samcheever.com/newsletter

ALSO BY SAM CHEEVER

If you enjoyed **Death and the Diva** you might also enjoy these other fun mystery series by Sam. To find out more, visit the **BOOKS** page at www.samcheever.com:

Grave Theatrics: For more fun with MayBell and Shakes!
Country Cousin Mysteries
Silver Hills Cozy Mysteries
Gainfully Employed Mysteries
Honeybun Heat Series
Mature Magic Paranormal Women's Fiction
Enchanting Inquiries Paranormal Cozy Mysteries
Yesterday's Paranormal Mysteries
Reluctant Familiar Paranormal Mysteries

ABOUT THE AUTHOR

USA Today and Wall Street Journal Bestselling Author Sam Cheever writes mystery and suspense, creating stories that draw you in and keep you eagerly turning pages. Known for writing great characters, snappy dialogue, and unique and exhilarating stories, Sam is the award-winning author of 100+ books.

To learn more about Sam and her work, visit her at one of her online hotspots:
www.samcheever.com
samcheever@samcheever.com

www.ingramcontent.com/pod-product-compliance
Lightning Source LLC
Chambersburg PA
CBHW060533260626
47161CB00003B/889